""When those in authority fail to reprove sin,
then often the good are punished
with the wicked."
-Heinrich Kramer, 1486 "Malleus Maleficarum"
(The Hammer of Witches)

The Watchman
Arla Dahl
Copyright © 2015 Arla Dahl

ISBN-13: 978-0-9904016-9-8

Published by Brooklyn Rose Press
All rights reserved
www.arladahl.com

Cover Illustration by Arla Dahl & Kolleen Shallcross.

Cover and Design by Kolleen Shallcross

TESTIMONIALS

"Governor Jameson Foster makes John Hathorne look like an incompetent fool in this well-crafted, wickedly erotic romp through witch trial hysteria. Arla Dahl will whet your appetite for more."
-- Candy Caine, author of contemporary interracial erotica

"Fifty Shades-meets-Shakespeare in this eloquent, erotic tale by Arla Dahl, where the author's wicked fantasy takes us to the final hours of a twisted Salem-ish witch trial, when The Watchman's flesh is put to the titillating test."
– Debra Druzy, Contemporary Romance Author

"Totally worth the wait! I've been chomping at the bit to read this final installment of Dahl's Immoral Virtue trilogy and it did not disappoint. We love her!!! The Watchman was so hot and satisfying, it's the perfect conclusion. We can't wait to find out what she's up to next."
– Chloe and Sabine's Smart Mouth Smut

"In Arla Dahl's erotic and immensely satisfying witch trial trilogy, every point on an accused's body is most thoroughly examined for the devil's mark. A witch feels no pleasure or pain, but an innocent feels everything, and passion prevails in the battle between good and evil."
– D. B. Shuster, author of the Neurotica series

ACKNOWLEDGMENTS

The Immoral Virtue Trilogy began as an exercise in creativity for me. I had always been moved by the trials of Salem Village, and when the muse demanded a new project, the twisted events of 1692 seemed worth twisting further.

 I am ever so thankful to my family and friends for their unwavering support of this project, and for their understanding as I locked myself away, day after day, to research and write these stories.

I had always heard, and always believed, writing to be a solitary act. I know now it could not be done, by me at least, without having you all within reach.

To each of you, all of you - and to Giles Scott for his unrelenting insistence that I tell this story his way - I will be forever grateful.

Immoral Virtue Trilogy
Arla Dahl

Book Three
The Watchman

"All witchcraft comes from carnal lust,
which is in women insatiable."
~Heinrich Kramer, 1486
"Malleus Maleficarum" (*The Hammer of Witches*)

DEDICATION

To those who came to the defense of the accused,
despite great risk to their own safety,
and to those who denounced the trials
for the farce they were.

x

FROM THE AUTHOR

Dear Reader,

Under Puritan rule in Salem Village during the 1600s, it was understood that a tangible and perpetual war raged between good and evil. In this war, every Puritan – man, woman and child – was a soldier for good, every Puritan soul, a battlefield.

Evil lurked everywhere, in the form of witches. They could be your neighbors, your wife, your mother, even a brave sea captain or soldier who fought for the colonies...

What was a devout Puritan to do? What would you have done? Join the majority and condemn the accused, uncertain now of their innocence? Or defend them and invite suspicion upon yourself?

What of the children imprisoned for months with their parents, like Dorcas Good, a girl of only four years. Badgered, was she, to confess the sins of her mother until her innocent mind crumbled beneath the burden.

Were that your child, would you not confess? What of the fate of your soul? For a lie, such as false confession, would damn it to eternal darkness. Yet to watch a child suffer for you...surely you would accept the fate of your soul to spare her that pain.

What if the suffering were yours alone? Like Giles Corey, a man of eighty years. He chose to endure an agonizing death rather than validate the court by answering to charges of witchcraft against himself.

A plea of innocence or guilt could have spared him death by Pressing. Yet to compromise, to give in to the wicked – his accusers, the courts and his torturers – would have been to dishonor himself and his name. Thus he, for honor and stubborn pride, perished. And the villagers sighed in relief.

In their search for the mark of the beast, in the darkest most secret spot upon the witch's body and soul, those of a most immoral virtue condemned the innocent. They stripped them and probed them and dishonored them beyond comprehension when, to find the blackest mark of all, the darkest evil of their time, all that was needed was a long, honest look at themselves.

May you be unmarked.

Arla

The Watchman

Arla Dahl

"…the Devil leaveth other marks upon their body,
sometimes like a blue spot, or red spot,
like a flea-biting;
sometimes the flesh sunk in and hollow…
all which for a time may be covered,
yea taken away,
but will come again, to their old form."
~ Michael Dalton, the Countrey Justice, 1618

Chapter One

Wedick Colony, 1682
– Two Hours to Moonset

The howl of cold wind thundered beneath shouts from the raucous mob amassed on the grounds of the governor's manor. Though daybreak would soon be upon them, darkness would linger, for fears of evil, of witches and cursed souls filled their hearts with dread.

Governor Jameson Foster stood with the watchman before him, his grip firm around the watchman's hands, bound at his back by Jameson himself. Though reluctant to see the watchman, his friend, at the crowd's mercy, he was honor-bound to see they had their fill, and duty-bound to examine his flesh for the devil's mark, as he had confessed to having lain with a witch.

Jameson glanced at Elizabeth Hobbs, herself accused as well. She stood naked still. Displayed for all. Yet her stubborn pride, pride which had helped to seal her fate, kept her head high. She had been examined by the crowd, then determined to have been marked by the beast and deemed a witch. He had little choice but to order her bound in the forest until dawn...

If not for the watchman's foolish heart, she would remain there now, not here, angering the crowd further. Had the watchman lain with Elizabeth, and she were marked as the crowd exclaimed, then he would be marked as well, for it was known a witch, ruled by Satan, could not control her evil lust, but would have need to spread it to one and all.

Jameson turned back to the crowd. They pushed forward, punched the air with their torches. Their fear and anger so fully absorbed only madness could rule their minds.

Seeing no way to quell their temper, Jameson pushed his friend closer to them. It was clear friendship, kinship and certainty of innocence would not prevent Giles Scott's examination this night. He would be roused, his desires awakened, stirred further then satisfied, for it is only the witch who cannot feel, who cannot be roused nor sated by a mere mortal hand.

Jameson drew a full breath and called out, "Be this a witch?"

Shouts of assent answered his bellowed question. As he knew they would. As he feared.

"Giles," Jameson said as the crowd jeered, demanding the watchman be stripped bare before them. "They seek blood this night."

"Aye." Giles stood rigid. Neither resisting nor cowering. He would bear the humiliation of the crowd's taunts and touches. And Jameson would permit it. He would require it for Giles as he had required it for the women who endured the same shame this night. Yet the vigor with which the crowd sought to examine him proved their judgment clouded, their minds believing only evil surrounded them. He would not subject his friend to that.

Jameson glanced up at the sky. Too soon dawn would be upon them, bringing with it final judgment of the accused.

"Come," he said and turned toward the manor, taking Giles with him. "You will follow," he said to Elizabeth, hating the sight of her at that moment, for it was her pride, her resistance, her foolery which had led his friend to this fate.

She took a step toward him as Samuel Stoughton burst from the crowd, his skinny pale fingers closing over Elizabeth's upper arm.

Giles lurched toward them, and Jameson hauled him back by a bound arm. "You are watchman no longer," he said low so only Giles would hear.

"She should be bound!" Samuel shouted in that hawkish barking way of his. "She should be spread before us all lest the mark fade and reappear from her flesh once more."

A rumble came from the crowd as the villagers debated Samuel's wisdom. Some were eager to see Elizabeth opened to their eyes again, some too frightened by the evil they believed lay deep within her heart.

Samuel tugged her back toward the platform where she had been spread and bound just an hour prior. Where the crowd had examined every inch of her flesh. Where her every crease and fold and orifice was tested for sensitivity by the crowd. And where they discovered the mark upon her thigh.

As Samuel dragged Elizabeth behind him, her bare feet slipped on the cold wet grass. Fear such as Jameson had not seen in her eyes this night shone bright, wild and pleading as she looked back at him. The extent of the crowd's cruelty no doubt still clear in her mind. She deserved punishment, but none such as this.

He turned away from the sight of her and gave voice to the crowd's fears. "You would have a witch bound before you? A witch who would render you, Samuel—as all men—either incapable or so lustful he cannot control himself, even if pigs or dogs be his only sheath?"

Shrieks of shock, and shouts of rage, came from the crowd as was Jameson's desire.

Samuel took Elizabeth closer to the platform. The shackles hanging from the beam that topped it clanked harshly with every blast of blustery air. "This witch will have no power over us," Samuel shouted as the crowd parted to let him pass. "Pious men cannot be harmed by the likes of her if she be bound."

Jameson strolled toward them, forcing a steady calm pace. "Were not today's sinners most pious a day prior?" he said, his tone measured yet firm for all to hear.

Samuel turned but said not a word, then turned back and continued on his way.

Elizabeth stumbled behind him. Up the platform stairs, toward the shackles. And she stood there, naked. Shivering. Her frightened gaze darting from one in the crowd to another. Her red hair, wild in the cold wind. Her bare flesh pale and spotty in the frigid night.

Yet she did not resist, did not struggle nor shield herself in any way. The fire in her heart doused... but why? She had refused to submit to Jameson earlier when he could have spared her this shame. When he could have sought to prove her innocence, taken his time with her examination. He would have touched her gently, not crudely as was the habit of this mob. He would have awakened her desires. He would have forced her to feel his touches, and to respond, for it is only the witch who cannot feel. And he would have been certain she felt his every caress. His every probe.

She would have craved it, sought release. And, had he proven her body unmarked by the beast, he would have granted her that release until he had drained every tremor from her body. Every spasm, every sigh, every lust-filled breath.

"'Tis the pious Satan most wishes to turn," Jameson said. "And 'tis Satan's pleasure witches seek to fulfill." He looked at the crowd, noted their fear, then settled his gaze on Samuel's, daring the insolent fool to challenge him further. Not speaking again until the moment Samuel drew his own breath for words. "Tell me, Samuel," Jameson said, "is it not Satan's desire to fill our hearts with lust?"

"Aye. 'Tis so."

"Then it would please him, would it not, to see men rendered incapable so they might leave their women yearning?" He did not wait for Samuel's response. "It would," he said, "for who better to seduce needy women than the greatest seducer of all?"

He let the crowd's nervous grumbling linger, then strode forward, climbed the platform stairs and snatched Elizabeth from Samuel's grasp.

"Nay." Jameson turned with her, back toward the manor. "All would be safer with her locked inside where I might keep close watch."

She hurried beside him, not struggling even in his grasp. Whereas before, a mere glance from him sent her pride soaring, her venomous words of resistance sealing her fate.

They reached Giles, and Jameson nudged him until Giles led the way up the manor steps.

Inside, Jameson tightened his grip on Elizabeth's arm and dragged her forward, resenting her for adding to the pain and chaos of this night. She struggled with him as she had not with Samuel, and he flung her from his grasp. She stumbled against the wall and he followed her, pressed his hand to her neck and held her there, pushing her further back to that wall.

"Your stubborn pride is to blame for what happens here now," he said.

"Dimwitted neighbors are to blame." She spat the words even as he clasped her neck tighter.

"Tis your resistance—"

"They confused time!" Her eyes, red from the cold, filled with tears, and he knew not the cause. Fear? Guilt? "They insisted I appeared in two places at once," she said, her gaze unwavering even as her tears spilled. "As myself, they said, and as my specter... yet you dare say I am to blame for what happens here?"

"Elizabeth."

Jameson turned at Giles' soft reproachful tone. His gaze was firmly on Elizabeth's. Heat and concern battling within it.

"Turn your back," Jameson said to his friend, unwilling to allow Elizabeth further rule over him in this moment.

Giles shifted as commanded, his quick glance at Jameson filled with sadness and resignation. Had Elizabeth indeed turned Giles toward darkness, Jameson would see to her punishment himself. It would be swift and complete.

He turned back to her, stood closer, nearly flattening her to the wall, his hand molded to the pale column of her throat, his forearm pressed between her naked breasts. "There is mischief this night, and a thirst for blood such as I have never seen," he said. "'Tis the work of darkness. 'Tis your work?"

She laughed as though crazed, and he tightened his hand to her neck, strangling the sound. He eased back then, and dropped his hand from her, letting his gaze drip over her body, naked and pale, her breasts heaving, her nipples hard. He dropped his gaze lower, to her unshaven mound. Giles swore, before all, he had examined her and found her unmarked. But how could he declare her so when part of her still lay veiled? Had he truly tested her or had she bewitched him?

Jameson captured her gaze once more.

With bold defiance, she met that gaze. "'Tis your fair hand you tout," she said and cringed as though the words left her mouth sour. "Your eyes they trust. How can you claim to uncover evil, which tricks the most diligent eye, yet fail to see madness so plain?"

Her every word rang true. It was madness. It was terror. It was fury. So many as accused would not be marked, to believe so was madness itself. Yet there were witches. He had condemned several this year. Two hanged, caught in the act. Murderers with blood on their hands, the others banished... he looked to Giles. Of course, those banished had not been driven to the edge of darkness with nothing but the clothes they wore. Jameson would not permit such cruelty, nor would Giles, who readily saw to their safety.

The manor doors opened and closed. Abigail. She had been through much this night. Herself accused, stripped before the crowd, examined by their lustful hands. Probed and tested by him. And though he proved her innocence and declared her free to leave, she remained, at his side, aiding in the examination of the others.

Her eyes showed pain as they looked to Elizabeth then to him. Did she, too, believe him blind?

"Evil is found when evil is sought," he said, to no one and to all. "I seek innocence."

He snatched Elizabeth's arm and dragged her along the hall beside him. He urged Giles ahead once again until they had entered his chamber. Abigail entered with them, closing the door behind her.

She had defended Elizabeth. Would still. And in truth, even he did not believe Elizabeth marked as sworn to by the crowd. But final decree of guilt or innocence was for him to declare, not for them. And not for Giles. The villagers trusted him to be fair and just. Giles…

He pressed his hand to Giles' shoulder, guided him toward the heat and light of the hearth. "Remain here," he said, not wishing to examine his friend. To force him to prove manly ability, to arouse him and to withhold release, to see that he endure the agonies of pleasure until such time as his - and thereby Elizabeth's - innocence was proven.

He turned from Giles, pulled Elizabeth behind him, so hard, she gasped and stumbled.

"Good Sir…"

Jameson glanced back at Abigail, unwilling, unable to permit her to stay his hand as she had tried many times this night. "See to Mercy," he said, aware Mercy remained, bound and alone in the other chamber for far too long. Her lust as yet unsated, her guilt or innocence as yet unclear. "Remove the clamps upon her," he said, facing Abigail directly now, holding her gaze, assuring himself she understood what she was to do. "You will not soothe her, Abigail, but permit her to feel every moment."

Abigail's lovely eyes widened, the memory of what Mercy would endure clear in her gaze. Though he had soothed Abigail when he had examined her, when he had clamped her breasts, her nipples as he had Mercy's, when he had felt Abigail tremble from the sudden pain as he removed those clamps and held her until she calmed, he would not permit the same for Mercy. Nay. Mercy would not permit it, for her pleasure differed in many ways. Ways Abigail had yet to learn.

"I will have your word," he said to Abigail.

She hesitated only a moment, then lowered her gaze to the floor. "I... shall do as you ask," she said and though he knew she would, he knew as well, she would feel the pain in her heart as Mercy felt it in her breasts.

He pointed to the door between chambers. "Take a candle from the hearth," he said and followed her with his gaze. He noted the slight tremor of her hand as she held the candle, the hesitant way she reached for the door. "Do not fear for her, Abigail," he said. "She fears not. That is my vow."

She faced him, innocence in her eyes. Despite all she had endured, all she had seen...by his hand, by those of the villagers...tenderness still ruled her, and tugged at something within him. He had bedded her. Her beauty and desire ruling him. And when he thought she had betrayed him, marked him, his hand had grown severe. She endured it all, his harsh fondling, forced probing...accepting it as much to prove her own innocence, it seemed, as to prove his. And then she forgave him for it.

A kinder heart he did not know. "You will go now," he said, well aware the others watched. "But remain no longer than is required, for Mercy, above all, takes pleasure from eyes upon her."

Abigail nodded slowly and he found himself looking her way even after she had closed the door between chambers.

He glanced toward Giles, whose gaze drifted from him to where Abigail had stood, then back again. The questions in his friend's eyes were many yet the time not right to answer. He had much to do and daybreak would not wait.

He took Elizabeth to the far wall where shackles lay ready, then secured her by one ankle, though he wished to mount her there more firmly. To force her to see the result of her resistance. To give her no choice but to see Giles bared, probed by Jameson's own hand. Aroused and held firmly at the edge of release until he throbbed. Pulsed with need so great he would beg Jameson to grip him harder, to stroke him faster and drain his seed, thus proving himself unmarked by the witch...

It was how it would be. For Giles, as for others Jameson had examined. Torturous pleasure meant to awaken, to prove the flesh unmarked, untouched by the numbing hand of evil.

He stood back from Elizabeth. Tempering his persistent desire to punish her. "Clasp your hands at your back," he said, then lowered his gaze to her breasts. So full, so lush. More so as she clasped her hands behind her and they were thrust out before him.

She was lovely, her flesh flawless, her body slight yet full. Her beauty marred only by her pride and the filthy lecherous hands of the villagers. Her taut belly bore scratches, her hips, gently rounded, held impressions of hands that gripped her too tight. 'Twas their way, the villagers, to show no mercy, like starved dogs with a single bone.

He captured her gaze with his own and she did not look away. He would waste no sympathies over what she endured, as it was her choice to resist his hand, and to submit to theirs.

"You will remain so, with your hands clasped, lest I be forced to bind you further." He glanced up at the restraints, mounted high and wide above her, giving no doubt to how he would spread her should she not obey.

Her gaze did not waver from his. "I do not wish to be bound so again."

He would think not. "When they touched you, Elizabeth," he said of the villagers, "when they bound you for their pleasure and spread you wide..." He lowered himself to one knee, there before her, to examine the spot where the crowd insisted the devil had placed his mark. "...were you roused by their hands?" Her skin was cool beneath his palm. "By their touches...and their insistent prodding?" The pale flesh of her inner thigh was soft beneath his hand as he pushed her leg wide so he might see the mark clearer. "Or were you cold and unfeeling...like the witch?" The mark lingered as before. Red. Bruising. As Giles had said, 'twas created by the cruel touch of the crowd, not by the beast as they had feared.

She did not answer and he stood, waited for her response.

She looked past him to where Giles stood bound, and Jameson turned to look at his friend. Giles drew a breath as to speak and Jameson silenced him with his glance.

He turned back to Elizabeth and she drew her own breath. He shushed her. "Think well, Elizabeth," he said, "for it was Giles who said you writhed in pleasure, and it was I, myself, who smelled the heady scent of your lust whence they had their fill..."

She opened her mouth but no words came forth.

"Do you deny it, Elizabeth? Do you deny you took pleasure from their lustful hands?"

Tears filled her eyes and she looked away.

He grasped her chin, made her face him again. "I will hear your answer."

She blinked and her tears fell. "I cannot deny it. I do not. I felt their every touch as was their want...I felt it all." A lovely pink flush rose, like a lazy wave, from her chest up to her face. The shame of pleasure given against her will, seeming to battle with her pride.

He released her, brushed her tears from her face with the back of his hand and felt the heat of her shame against him. It was not a small feeling of pleasure he took from her discomfort, for a witch rarely felt such humility. Nay, the witch would prefer to have others humbled and shamed before her...

"And is it your pleasure now, Elizabeth," he stood back from her just an inch, "to see Giles here, eager to submit to me in your stead?"

"Nay."

Without warning, he cupped his hand to her core, and tangled his fingers in the thick coarse hair that hid secrets he believed Giles had not examined well enough. He was pleased by her sudden gasp, though unmoved by the shock in her eyes. Deftly, he spread her nether lips and stroked his longest finger against her.

Her body trembled, her breaths came hard and harsh, yet she did not release her hold on her hands at her back. Showing more control than he believed her to possess.

She was free of desire. Dry. Cold. Though witches were known to deceive, this proof, at least could not be denied, and for that he was pleased, for Giles' coming shame did not rouse her.

He dropped his hand from her. Turned to Giles, his friend, who should not be there at all, and saw the familiar determined set to his jaw, and a fire in his eyes. Giles Scott. Watchman, protector.

Not once but always, Giles averted his eyes while in this chamber, respectful of the women so bared and bound. Not once, never, had he succumb to the pleasure of an accused, save for now, with Elizabeth.

Jameson went to his friend. "Such concern," he said and reached for the ropes holding Giles' arms at his back. "'Tis layered deeper within you than I have seen." Was it lust…true desire…or bewitchment?

Jameson looked at Elizabeth as he untied the ropes binding his friend and saw her gaze solid on Giles as though they two shared silent words. He tossed the ropes onto the long wide table beside them then leaned closer to Giles. "How did you come to examine her?" Had she enticed him so he might do her bidding, or marked him as was a witch's need…

He circled Giles then, stood between him and Elizabeth. "I would know the answer."

"'Twas not my place to do…"

"Nay, it was not." Jameson waited for more from his friend, eager to know what drew Giles to soothe such yearnings for an accused. Jameson himself had been tempted many a times, yet succumbed only this night, and only to Abigail.

He glanced toward the door to the chamber where she tended Mercy. Concerned there were no cries from Mercy as yet…

He wished to condemn no one this night...not Mercy, not even Elizabeth...but most of all not Giles. He closed his eyes, hating the very thought.

At Giles' silence, he turned to his friend, stepped aside so he would see Elizabeth fully. "Was it her lovely form?" He looked at her himself. Wondered over her hold on Giles, taking him from his role of watchman, for which he was most honorable, to that of accused. Could it be her beauty alone? "Was it her pleasured keening that stirred you, Giles?" he said softly, "Was it the flush of her body beneath the touch of the crowd?"

Jameson went to her then. "Tell me," he said as he stood behind her, "how did you examine her?" He touched his hands to her waist. She gasped at the contact and he hushed her, kept his gaze on Giles and trailed his fingertips from Elizabeth's waist to her hips, her flesh silken beneath his touch. "Did you hold her breasts in your hands..." He grazed his hands upward, lightly cupped her breasts, stroked them with his fingertips. Each brush of them drawing a deeper breath from her.

He dropped his gaze lower upon Giles. Nary a twitch of arousal presented beneath his snug breeches despite Elizabeth's beauty and his handling of her. Had she marked him, stolen his ability, as witches were want to do?

He stroked lower to Elizabeth's hips. Cupped a hand to one, smoothed his palm back to her rump, molding it to her softness. He pushed her slightly, turned her so Giles might clearly see his hand upon her.

"Did you strike this tender flesh, Giles..." He drew his hand back, smacked her lovely rump and took pleasure in her gasp. He let her sweet rounded flesh jiggle then smoothed his hand over it in slow, gentle circles, "…did you strike it with your palm or with a switch?"

"Nay…"

Jameson pressed his free hand to her belly to steady her, then tightened the other against her rump, squeezing until her whole body tensed and she huffed an angry breath. Testing her he was, and testing Giles. Pleased Elizabeth neither spoke nor released her clasped hands.

"Did you probe her…Giles? Test her most secret spots?" Ignoring her small whimper at his words, he soldiered his fingers and slid them deep between her cheeks, brushing the side of them against all of her tender and guarded places. She tensed further, locking his hand there where he knew she most wished it not to be.

At Giles' silence, Jameson looked up. His friend's gaze, seething with fury Jameson did not recognize, held his. Concern clenched Jameson's chest as a new understanding dawned. He took his hand from Elizabeth. Certain she had compelled Giles to examine her, to fool his eye so he might defend her as now. Jameson would know the truth. Demand it. Wrest it from one or the other.

"Did you do her bidding, Giles?" He turned her to face Giles, locked his hand around hers clasped at her back. "Did you examine her upon her request…or did you answer your own need?"

"'Twas in answer to her request," Giles said, his shoulders squared, his voice firm, with no shame or regret. "And by my own will."

Jameson released Elizabeth with a shove that made her stumble. He went to Giles. His concern for his friend greater now for he had admitted to doing Elizabeth's bidding. Jameson's greatest hope was to find Giles unmarked, though doubt now pained him deeply. "It is by your own will...as well...that you submit to me this hour?"

"Aye. 'Tis."

He had vowed Elizabeth would go free should he prove Giles unmarked. Yet, had she bewitched him...marked him... "I would see all of you, Giles."

A muscle worked in his jaw. "Aye."

"I would rouse you as – "

"As you would rouse her...yet only I submit." Giles' gaze did not waver nor show a hint of doubt. He stood proud, though not prideful. Confident.

Jameson looked back at her. 'Twas too much a pleasure, the sight of her. A splendid gift of nature. Perhaps, he would hope, she had not bewitched Giles so much as stirred his heart, much as Abigail stirred his own.

He turned then, toward the door between chambers. Listened, for a brief moment, for any moan or murmur from within. He heard nothing beyond the snap from the logs in the hearth beside Giles, and the rasp of their breaths, each of them, at their own pace.

Had Abigail removed the clamps as he had said, then even one such as Mercy would cry out. He went to the large chest that held all he needed to examine the accused and withdrew a large tow-cloth pouch containing implements for testing one such as Mercy. A large, hollowed stone phallus, delicate chains and heavier ones, leather restraints...the oils...for use on Giles as well...

He set it all on the wide table beyond Giles, fearful now for Mercy's innocence, for surely the clamps, once removed, would cause her great pain...

Lest she be a witch able to feel nothing at all.

He turned to Giles. Gave only a passing glance toward Elizabeth, too aware how swiftly dawn approached. "We begin," he said.

Giles nodded.

"Why are you here, Giles Scott?"

"To prove my word true. I, as Elizabeth, am unmarked."

"And you accept your fate this hour?" It was the question he had to ask, the question Elizabeth denied, while the others –

"Aye. For to prove my innocence will prove her innocence as well."

Jameson gave Giles a single nod. "As will your guilt, prove her –"

A scream, more like a hoarse choking cry, came from the other chamber. Mercy.

Jameson closed his eyes. Breathed a small sigh of relief, then looked at Giles again, eager to continue this. To finish.

Giles' eyes were wide in confusion. Horror. His breath seemed held as he looked toward the other chamber. And though Jameson understood the anger and accusation in Giles' eyes when he faced him again, Jameson would not explain his treatment of Mercy. Not with dawn so soon to arrive and with so much more to do.

He locked his gaze on Giles', leaving no doubt to the severity of the coming moments. "It is time, Giles," Jameson said. "Disrobe."

The Watchman

Chapter Two

Abigail had hesitated when she stepped into the other chamber. Though she examined Mercy earlier, she had failed to arouse her. That failure brought pain to Mercy now. Pain Jameson warned Abigail not to soothe.

She blinked into the darkness. Candles flickering on the far wall outlined Mercy's naked form in a faint glow. Her body swayed, stretched as she was, with her ankles shackled to the floor, and her arms bound well above her head. The rope binding her wrists was pulled taut through a bolt in the ceiling and down to another mounted on the wall.

A leather strap, secured to that rope, passed through irons clamped on her nipples. Without slack, it pulled her that way as well, forcing Mercy to teeter on her toes to relieve the strain on her arms and her breasts, while stretching them if she flattened her feet to the floor, the unyielding clamps merciless, either way, as they gripped her.

Though not bound so brutally, Abigail remembered the biting pain of those clamps. The warm numbing sensation that replaced the pain as time wore on. And the pain, shocking in its strength, when Jameson removed the clamps and sensation had returned, making those tiny bits of her body throb and burn until she felt she could bear it no longer. She had cried out with the shock of it and he had soothed her, laved his tongue over her, subduing the pain, holding her. Kissing her...

Mercy laughed. A small moist sound of wicked pleasure. "You have been sent to tend me in his stead." She sighed, danced on her toes. Then she tilted her face up to the ceiling and her hair fell freely behind her in wild array.

Abigail set the candle upon a small chest a yard within the room, then went to Mercy. "I am to remove the clamps," she said.

A harsh breath gushed from deep within Mercy's chest, deflating it, her nipples stretched further.

"I...fear..." Abigail said, "...you will feel great pain."

Mercy looked at her then, a smile in her eyes. "None such as I have not felt before," she said. "I regret only that it is you and not he who will do it."

"You would have our governor see your pain?"

"I would have him see my pleasure."

Abigail could only stare in horror, frightened by the lengths Mercy would go for Jameson's attentions. "'Tis a foolish desire," she said, wishing reason would light upon Mercy. "These moments will not bring pleasure."

"Pleasure or pain...I wish to feel it." Fatigue strained Mercy's voice. "Only the witch cannot." Exertion hardened her breaths. "'Tis time," she said. "If it be his bidding you would do, then do it now."

Abigail reached for the clamps. Unsure if the pain of removing one then the other would be more merciful than both together. She released one, let it drop and its weight pulled the other. She waited, breath held, remembering well that instant of relief when she had believed the worst had passed, and then –

Mercy screamed, a thick and harsh sound, as though the scream itself caused great pain. She flailed about upon her toes, her breaths heaving, the remaining clamp still latched to her nipple, straining, tugging.

Abigail knew. Remembered the agony of blood rushing back to that part of her. She ached to comfort Mercy but could not, for Jameson's warnings were clear.

She reached for the other clamp. Felt not the slightest satisfaction at Mercy's pain, not the slightest pleasure, despite Mercy's shameless yearnings for Jameson. 'Twas not the time for such feelings...

Abigail closed her eyes, admonishing herself for indulging her jealousies, then as now, for Mercy, like the others, had not chosen this fate.

She removed the second clamp.

Mercy stilled, then her breaths grew quick. Gruff. And then she screamed again and the sound was like that of a tortured soul. Abigail reached for her as she writhed about upon her toes, her arms taut above her. Her head lagged forward then back as her dance of pain spun her to and fro.

Abigail ran her hands over Mercy's body, smoothing easily over her waist, her hips, down her thighs. She did not dare touch Mercy's breasts now. Did not soothe the pain in her nipples. Merely tried to distract her with light caresses over her belly, firm grips to her thighs, comforting Mercy in her own way, without betraying Jameson's trust.

She circled Mercy as Mercy swayed, and brushed her hands over Mercy's back, her shoulders. The flesh was cold and damp beneath her touch. She tried to warm it, gliding both hands over the swell of Mercy's buttocks, no longer caring how Mercy had gazed at Jameson. Only caring that she not be made to suffer more to prove her innocence.

Mercy calmed some, though her breaths remained harsh, her body all but hanging from the ropes above her.

"Does the pain linger still?" Abigail asked, surprised by Mercy's response. A moan. Soft. Light. The sound of contentment. Not fear, nor suffering.

Jameson's words came back to her. "*'Tis not everyone who fears punishment*," he had said. Was it so for Mercy?

Hesitantly, Abigail scraped her fingernails over Mercy's buttocks. Mercy tensed and Abigail scratched the flesh harder, leaving light reddish trails behind. Mercy gasped, balanced on her toes as she inched first away then toward the touch as though seeking more.

If these touches brought pleasure, then perhaps Abigail's earlier touch had been too gentle... Perhaps that was how she failed Mercy when she had tried to examine her then, to arouse her.

Yet, how much stronger must the hand be to please Mercy?

She circled her again. Mercy's nipples were angry red, sore to sight even in that dim light. Abigail reached up, glancing only briefly at Mercy's eyes, now lowered and focused upon hers. Waiting, almost pleading. Showing more desire now than in the entire time Abigail had caressed and probed her earlier, with gentle touches, gentle prodding.

Before Jameson witnessed Abigail's failure and brought Mercy here, to be further tested. By his knowing hand.

Abigail would learn what Mercy craved. Perhaps then she might prove Mercy's innocence. And perhaps then Jameson would send Mercy from this place to be fully clothed once again.

Gently she touched a single finger to each of Mercy's tender nipples. Mercy hissed in a breath but did not pull away. And Abigail pressed the firm heated nubs harder, following Mercy as she then teetered back and away from the touch.

"This pains you?" she asked, and eased the pressure until her fingers barely brushed the hot pebbled surface.

"Nay," Mercy said on a sigh, "'Tis pleasure alone." She swayed, her body inching toward Abigail's fingertips.

Abigail rolled Mercy's nipples lightly between her fingers, aware of the heated path, a path of need, that such a touch created. Yet aware, as well, how sore they would be from the clamps. It could not be pleasure alone but pain...though perhaps such that the two felt as one? Lightly, she pulsed her fingers to them as Jameson had done to her, and the same need and moist gushing heat filled her now as then, though her breasts, fully clothed, remained untouched...

Mercy moaned, a gruff sound.

Abigail's own moan came hard from within her chest, echoing Mercy's. Where she had failed before, she succeeded now, and could do more... then Jameson would not need to leave Giles. She needed only his permission to continue.

She stood closer to Mercy, shared her heat, gave and took as Mercy's body warmed. She cupped the sides of Mercy's breasts, smoothed her palms up slowly, inch by inch along Mercy's raised arms, higher until she could reach no more. Mercy's fingers laced with hers and their breasts pressed flat to each other's. Mercy's softness against Abigail, an unfamiliar feeling, stole her breath. "I wish to release you," Abigail said, her voice a whisper, "but I cannot."

"You will not," Mercy said on a warm breath Abigail felt against her cheek. "For you wish more to please him…and him alone." She smiled then. "Do you wish as well that he might please you?"

Abigail dropped her hands from Mercy and stood back, felt both chilled and heated. Perhaps not Mercy's wrists but her tongue should be bound for such a bold retort.

"I wish to not see you bound so," Abigail said, her chin lifting as Mercy's smile grew. "Yet…your innocence must still be proved." She turned away, retrieved the candle she had set on the chest, not wishing to endure further branding beneath Mercy's caustic tongue. "Until such time…" She headed toward the door to Jameson's chamber. "… you shall remain as you are."

"I shall remain this way or that," Mercy said, her voice soft, her words sharp. "And I shall accept what tests our dear governor might devise."

Abigail turned back, not wanting to hear more, yet needing to.

"I have no choice, for I would have him prove my innocence." Mercy turned to Abigail, inching about on her toes as far as the shackles would allow. "Though I fear, dear Abigail, as I writhe beneath his touch you will instead wish for proof of my guilt."

Words lodged within Abigail's throat and she could not speak, only mouth the shock she felt. Perhaps she should seek Jameson's permission, and rouse Mercy fully. With her own touches, she would prove Mercy unmarked, then urge Jameson to send her away.

Abigail rushed from the room, Mercy's soft laughter filling her ears even as she closed the door between them.

She breathed in the scent of need and fragrant oils which lingered still within Jameson's chamber. It calmed her, familiar as it was.

"You dawdle, Giles, when you know what is required."

Abigail turned at the impatience in Jameson's tone.

He stood before the table where she and all the other accused this night had been spread, naked and bound, so he might examine them closely. His blade had been sharp, his hand steady as he shaved each so he might see them fully. And now, Giles stood facing him. Back perfectly straight. Shoulders the same height as Jameson's. The breadth of both men, impressive. Powerful. Equal. Neither towering before the other. Neither cowering. Yet Jameson's authority thickened the air around him, made it quiver around her even as his gaze remained solid on Giles.

And then Giles' gaze shifted. Dropped from Jameson's and touched on Abigail as she stood, breath held, with her back to the door. He turned away slowly then, to look toward Elizabeth, herself still bound and bare, at the far wall.

How long Jameson would permit such dallying Abigail did not know, nor did she wish to learn.

She hurried to Giles' side. She had assisted the others, had helped them disrobe when fear had frozen them. But they were women, all. Familiar. She glanced at Jameson. His gaze, steady on her, neither strayed nor bore evidence of his thoughts. And then he gave her a small nod, urging her to progress as with the others.

"Giles?"

He turned his head toward her, only slightly, his lowered gaze not meeting her own.

"There is not time." She moved to stand at his back. "Dawn comes, and judgment with it." Her hands trembled as she lifted them toward the leather at his shoulders, offering a silent plea he would not resist as she removed his jerkin. "We must make haste." Her fingers closed over it and he startled, his body tensed, his powerful arms flexed, the muscles seeming almost painfully taut.

She drew back. Jameson inched closer. Confusion, not anger, in his eyes as he studied Giles.

"You have chosen this." He spoke the words slowly. A question...nay...a challenge, wrapped around each. "Of your own accord."

Silence passed between the two men, and Abigail held her breath, fearing Jameson's impatient wrath should Giles resist now.

And then tension left Giles all at once, as though the acceptance of his fate had finally filled him. "Aye."

He shifted then, and reached for the buttons on his jerkin. He eased each slowly through its tightly sewn opening, from the top where the sleeveless leather stretched wide over his chest, toward the middle where it lay fitted to his waist, and on to the bottom where it cinched some above his hips.

And though he hesitated as the last button broke free, he then dropped his arms to his sides, permitting her to draw the leather over his shoulders and down his arms. She bared his back, so broad and –

With a gasp, she saw him clearer. His back ravaged by vicious, welt-like scars. They crisscrossed every which way, down the length, across the breadth of him. Barely a scrap of untouched flesh lay bared. Her grip tightened to the warm leather she held, crushing it, her hands trembling, herself unable to look away from the horror before her.

Tears filled her eyes, mercifully obscuring the sight. And a whimper she could not withhold tore from her throat like a scream too frightened to be heard.

CRNO

Jameson's gaze held Giles'. His body tense in response to Abigail's horror. His fear for his friend greater than any he had felt before.

"Be thee marked, Giles?" He forced the question, the words as painful to speak as to hear.

"Aye."

"Nay!" Abigail trembled violently beside Giles, her tears spilling, his jerkin hugged tight to her breast as though a shield.

And then Jameson stood closer to his friend, lowered his eyes to Giles' bare chest, and saw it, the long healed slice and peel scars of whip against flesh.

He touched one ribbon like welt at the muscle of Giles' breast. "What punishment was this?"

"'Twas encouragement," Giles said, "so I might bear witness against another."

Jameson dropped his hand, knew well the horror of Giles' youth. His mother accused when he was but a new man of twelve, he and his brothers questioned…but never did Jameson suspect this, for never once had Giles spoken of such brutalities against himself. "Did you bear witness?"

"Nay." Giles' voice was thick. Gruff. "She was innocent." He looked to Elizabeth, his gaze lingering a moment before he lowered it.

Jameson turned to her - her gaze fixed on Giles. Her eyes wide as though pained. Shocked. The scars clearly new to her. Had Giles examined her, had he lain with her as he had said, then he had not exposed himself fully, for if he had, she would know of their existence…

Abigail's soft weeping drew Jameson to her. He cupped his hands to her small shoulders, and eased her to the stool beside the hearth. He could not offer soothing words for only fury at the injustice filled his mind. He forced gentleness to his hands, took Giles' jerkin from Abigail's grip and laid it upon her lap. And then he closed his eyes, doing all to prepare for what he would next see.

He went back to Giles. Circled his friend. Swallowed the rage building within him. Thinking of the child Giles had been, of others suffering the same plight. Their young flesh torn from them as the whip descended again and again. And all in the name of good over evil.

He forced his gaze over the length of Giles' back. Counted ten strokes. Twenty. The suffering unimaginable to him. "You are marked so elsewhere, Giles?" he asked, though he knew the answer for the lick of scars sliced down Giles' back to disappear beneath his breeches.

"Aye."

"I will see more."

Tension fixed Giles's stance yet further, as though he thought to resist. Jameson would spare him, but much would be done this night, much more than simple baring.

"Giles." He meant his tone to hold tenderness, understanding Giles' trepidation. Yet Giles had chosen this, to submit to this examination, so he might spare Elizabeth.

Giles bent to remove his boots, and despite the scars, muscles rippled across his back, the power of the man Jameson called friend, still an impressive sight. Boots to the side, Giles hesitated only a moment before he let his breeches fall, displaying the long-healed scars across his muscular buttocks and thighs.

Chest hurting from hard pounding within, Jameson circled Giles, noting the few but vivid marks left on his belly, the front of his thighs, his shins, the whip having been wielded so callously, so carelessly, it wrapped around his body to lick those parts of him as well.

Giles' manhood hid within its thick nest and Jameson feared what damage might have been done there as well. He touched a mark crossing above Giles' nipple. Drew his fingers along its length. "Do they pain you still?"

Giles stood unmoving, his gaze solid on Jameson's. "'Tis not pain," he said, "yet even a touch, slight and fleeting, shocks."

Jameson drew his hand away, cupped it to Giles' shoulder, slid it slowly down his arm. "There lies no mark here," he said, noting no scars, only unblemished flesh and solid muscle. "Your arms were spared?"

"They were bound. Well above."

"Giles…" Jameson shook his head, wanting to end this examination now. Not take it further. Knowing he had no choice but to continue. Though never would he torture an accused. Never would he allow such on his watch. "'Tis my wish to prove innocence through pleasure, not guilt through pain, 'tis why…" He glanced at Abigail as she wiped tears from her face. "…'tis why I must continue. If I do not, another shall take my place, and I will have naught to say in the manner of their hand."

Giles closed his eyes, seeming to consider Jameson's words. Then looked at Jameson with clear resolve.

"Test me as you will." He clasped his hands at his naked back. "I shall bear it now as before," he said. "And I shall prove there be no witches here."

Chapter Three

Jameson glanced at Elizabeth though not as Giles had. Nay, not with affection, for only she held the power to spare Giles this shame and pain.

Jameson went to the hearth, took the kettle from within and settled it beside Giles. He would examine his friend. Bring about his pleasure so all would see the truth of his words, that there be no witches.

"Abigail." Concern still etched her lovely face. "Fetch the wide cloth from the chest," he said, then turned to retrieve the blade and cloths from the shelf above the long table. He would make quick work of this. He would bare Giles fully and learn whether scars marred his manhood as well, or whether that part of him had been spared the whip.

He closed his eyes in silent reprimand. Though where the whip strayed should not be his concern, it was, for Giles…his friend…had endured much.

Jameson drew a breath, long and full. Marked was Giles by evil indeed, though whether the mark of the beast marred his flesh as well, Jameson would now learn.

He turned with the blade in his hand.

Giles' sharp inhale made his body rigid, and his gaze fixed upon the steel as it glinted in the firelight.

Jameson slowed his step, having never seen such fear in his friend's eyes. He looked at the blade he held, cool sharpened steel he used on all the accused. It bared them. Revealed secrets not permitted within these walls as he used it to whisk away every coarse hair, every fine strand, leaving nothing behind to veil their most protected and private parts.

It frightened them all, as would be expected, but none knew him as well as Giles.

With no choice, he eased closer to his friend. "You fear my hand?" he asked softly.

"Nay."

He permitted the lie, aware Giles ached to make it true. Each long drawn breath that filled Giles' chest, seemed to calm him, steady him, though they eased the fear in his eyes by none.

"'Tis good." Jameson set the blade and cloths on the stool by the hearth, taken by his friend's fear, his hand now unsteady on the blade. He drew closer to Giles, blocking his view of the sharpened steel. "'Tis not fear I would have you feel, my friend." He flattened his palm to Giles' hard chest, felt the heat and rapid thud beneath it.

Giles' gaze met Jameson's and in it Jameson saw the trust he sought.

"Abigail," he said, not looking from Giles. "Fetch the large amber vial as well." He kept his hand upon Giles as he stood behind him, stroking his hand from Giles' chest to his shoulder. The long-healed scars still angry, cruel. The slash of the whip slicing the flesh a vivid sight within his own mind. Did the sound, the sting or the smell of blood haunt Giles' dreams to this day? Or had he, the man he now was, quelled all thoughts to that time?

Abigail stood beside Jameson, her tiny smile as she looked up at him, fleeting. Heartening.

He reached for her, wanting to cup her sweet face in his hand, to thank her for her tender concerns. She tipped her head toward his palm, seeming to crave the same contact, though he granted the moment to neither of them.

Instead, he took the cloth from her and folded it into a long thick strip. He leaned toward his friend, careful not to let his doublet brush the long-healed wounds upon his back.

"Trust my hand is not meant to harm," he said, and settled the cloth over Giles' eyes, knotting it securely behind his head. Wishing for him to know only that which would arouse him. A whispered touch. A firm caress. By Jameson's hand or Abigail's, Giles would not be sure. Could not resist. Jameson would be certain of that for the sake of Giles' life.

Giles merely stood taller, brave in his posture. Silent with his thoughts.

Jameson took the vial from Abigail, poured its oil into his hand and hers, then set it into the pouch at his hip.

"'Tis not pain I will provide." He cupped his oiled hands to Giles' strong shoulders, used his fingers to ease the sudden tension. "'Tis pleasure."

He ran one hand down the length of Giles' arm. Slowly stroking the swell of well-hewn muscle, the tendons and veins. Feeling only the solidness of the man, nothing odd to mar his flesh, no demon's scars.

His hand reached Giles' fist and he forced it open, pressed his own fingertips to the palm.

Giles remained stiff, tight, and Jameson laced their fingers, caressing his thumb over the back of Giles' hand, his wrist. Forcing the tension from it before stroking upward along his arm again. "Only pleasure, Giles. I assure you." He spoke softly, his tone as low as the light from the hearth. Warm. As for all the accused, though perhaps more tender for Giles.

He examined his friend's other arm. With his eyes, his hands. Firmly, slowly drawing his hand down, feeling the tension, the power there. Then lower to pry open Giles' other tight fist.

All those he examined had felt fear. Women and men. All anticipated his touch, many unsure how to respond. Some timid and hesitant. Others eager to feel. Passion. Pain. Anything to prove innocence. Never had one remained so still. So rigid. Though he wished to ease the fear of his friend, he knew of no way but through these touches.

He shifted, held his palm, fingers splayed, an inch from Giles' marred back. He did not touch the flesh there, yet felt the heat of it, the heat of Giles.

It warmed his hand as he waved it slowly down the long, wide breadth of his back. Feeling without touching. Awakening without probing. Holding steady, a finger's width from Giles' flesh. Taking Giles' heat. Replacing it with his own.

Abigail's small cool hand covered his at Giles' back. Her gaze, one of patient encouragement. As though she knew how he feared hurting his friend, how he wished his touch would not shock but please.

The pressure of her hand, insistent though slight, urged his closer to Giles. One finger, the middle, touched, and Giles hissed in a quick breath.

With her hand still upon his, Jameson trailed his finger along one gnarled scar, whispering it down its length from Giles' shoulder to the middle of his back. And then, as slowly, as gently, he traced upward again.

Giles' muscles rippled as he tensed and flexed, seeming to shrink from each gentle stroke. One finger. Light and steady. The faintest brush down the full length of another scar. Pleasure or pain for a tortured man?

Not for a breath did Giles ease his stance. Not once did he speak or reveal thoughts to flee even as Jameson awakened these wounds and the memories of them. Giles' strength, his bravery, admirable. His fear compelling, for a true witch felt none.

Jameson glanced at Elizabeth, and then Abigail, beside him. Her small warm hand still upon his. The women he examined, all, suffered. Their terror not blurred by tortures of the past, yet plain and clear. They, too, bore it. Abigail...brave even as he accused her of deceit, forced her to feel more and more again. To prove herself unmarked.

And Elizabeth. Elizabeth who denied herself the safety of these chambers and suffered a worse fate at the hands of the villagers. Hands that would have stolen innocence from Abigail. Sweet innocence of heart.

He turned back to Giles, hating these marks upon his flesh. Hating the man who set them there.

He followed the path of the deepest scar. Stroked lower. Then lower still. Brushing his fingertip between the small dimples at the lowest part of Giles' back, and then over the slight swell of Giles' rump. Feather light, from the center to one side.

Giles stirred, clenched his buttocks, and Jameson allowed himself a small smile. The touch was felt, well and good. For the witch, 'twould not be so.

He stroked back to the middle again and on to the other side, brushing over scars and unmarred flesh alike. Pained to know his friend had hidden this truth from him despite their talks, their sharing of regret and anger over these tests. The injustices. The fate of Giles' mother…

Not once had Giles confided this torture.

Jameson stood back then. Breathed deeply. Wanting as much to know who would do such things to a young boy as to never learn his name, for surely he would take a whip to that man's hide himself.

"Good Sir?" Abigail gave his hand a light squeeze. Too aware was she of his hesitancy.

With her hand still upon his, he cupped Giles' buttocks, molding his palm over the cool flesh there. Gliding across the swell of one cheek to the other, his fingertips dripping into the crevasse between them, the oils upon his hand leaving a glistening path behind. Giles remained still, seemed not to breathe.

Jameson turned his hand, set Abigail's beneath his, formed it over the firmness of Giles' rump. Smoothed lower, pressing her hand where rump met thigh. Probed the muscle there. Squeezed the firm cheek. The heel of their hands tugging, spreading it slightly, easing back. Probing again until the muscles there flexed and twitched in the slightest response.

He released Abigail's hand to cup the other side with his own, kneading the firm taut flesh, warming it. His caresses and Abigail's spreading Giles' cheeks wide. A silent reminder of what Giles' knew well, that no part of him would remain unseen, untouched, untested.

"You feel these touches, Giles, my hand and Abigail's." He touched a hand to Giles' belly, smoothed it lower, into the nest of thick curls. Pressing, caressing lower still, until Jameson's pinky brushed the base of Giles' still-flaccid cock. It twitched at the touch but remained soft and all but hidden. "Her flesh against yours supple, her touch light, and gentle."

Jameson brushed against Giles' cock again, a slow drag of his finger across its base, combing through the dark thatch. "Mine, as your own..." He angled his hand in a caress, strong and firm, down the muscled length of Giles' thigh, then used the same strength to stroke upwards again, toward Giles' hip. "Our touch upon ourselves, knowing. What brings pleasure, what brings release..." The ridge and valley of random coarse hair and scars tickled Jameson's palm, yet no marks beyond those scars marred Giles' flesh. No teat nor further hint of evil's touch. "Is it the same for you as for me, Giles? I will know."

There was more to see, more to test. More to touch. For Giles' manhood lay, as yet, unmoved.

"I would reach all of you," Jameson said, and passed his thumb over Giles' cock. Slowly from base to tip, the flesh still soft, asleep when it should at least stir. "Stand wide, Giles, for I will do so now."

A full breath inflated Giles' chest before he slowly adjusted his stance. And Jameson curled his fingers over Giles' sac, ignoring the expected hiss of surprise. He held Giles loosely, lifted, stroked his thumb over the few coarse hairs there. Noted the new unsteady rhythm of Giles' breaths. Shorter. Sharper.

"'Tis fear alone you feel," he said, soft by Giles' ear. "Anticipation as well." He tightened his grip slightly, steadily, surely, feeling Giles tense further. "'Tis not pain you feel at this touch Giles, I know this well myself." He gentled his hold, dabbled his fingertips over each testicle, then along the ridge between them, noting the strain still upon Giles' face. His nostrils flared, his teeth clenched, lips parted. Prepared for pain Jameson vowed would not come. Fearing…feeling… every slight probe, every breath-like stroke. As was Jameson's wish.

Giles calmed only when Jameson eased his hand from Giles' thick hot sac.

"Abigail." He move to Giles' other side. "Take the blade from the stool."

Giles shifted, turned his head as to follow their movements. Aware. Alert behind the blind.

Jameson stood closer to his friend. Lowered his voice until he felt it pulse within his own chest. "You will be bared fully now, Giles."

A muscle twitched in his jaw. Nothing more.

Abigail held the blade to Jameson but he did not take it. His hand not yet steady.

Instead, he cupped his hand to Giles' thigh. Watching closely. Securing his other hand to Giles' shoulder. Calming him as he flinched at the touch. Giles' breath, a harsh gush of concern.

"Giles." Jameson spoke softly. "Have I harmed any in my care?" He stroked his hand downward over Giles' thigh, gripping the solid muscle there, feeling only the intense heat of his friend. He stroked upward again. Over Giles' hip, his palm firm and flattened to Giles' flesh as he swept it toward his belly, slowly stroking upward to his chest. And there, again, was the hard, quick thud of concern. "Giles."

"None have been harmed."

"Clasp your hands at your back."

With measured slowness, Giles did as told, and Jameson took the blade from Abigail. "Do not let go," Jameson said, and switched the blade so the spine brushed the curve of Giles' shoulder.

Giles tensed. Flinched. And Jameson drew the spine of the blade lower, along the tender back of his neck, walking slowly behind him. Barely grazing his flesh. Sending ripples of sensation over him.

"Nor shall you move," he said, the spine at Giles' other shoulder. "For should you do so..." Then down, gingerly, steadily, over Giles' chest. His gaze on the heavy rise and fall of it as Giles struggled to remain still, to calm his breaths, to ease his stance, for tension so great could not be held for long. "I will be forced to secure you." Jameson drew the spine lower, along the thin line from Giles' belly to his groin. Had it been the blade, it would scratch the flesh, whisk away the hairs, sparse though coarse. Awaken the senses.

He drew it lower still, into the thick mat there. Stroking over it, readying Giles for what was to come. "Must I restrain you, Giles? Or is your wish to remain still by will alone?" With one long slow stroke down the length of Giles' disinterested cock, Jameson looked for some sign of awareness. He saw none but for the slightest flick, Giles' fear too great.

He set the blade back on one stool and waved Abigail to the other, his hands on her shoulders, silently bidding her to sit before Giles.

Understanding made her tense but time would not permit her timidity now. He forced her to the stool, ignored the pleading in her eyes.

"You will answer," he said to Giles. "Or I will choose for you."

"It is by my will I am here," Giles said, his posture softening as neither hand nor steel touched him. "By my will alone, I shall remain."

Jameson took a heavy cloth from the stool and plunged it into the kettle of warm water. Soaking it fully, then squeezing the excess out.

How many had he examined? Tens, hundreds. Each ashamed to be bared in this way, every hair from their bodies whisked away. His hands on them, palpating, pulling, pinching. As he would do now with Giles' cock and scrotum, seeing them well, testing them for any unnatural mark or sign of the witch.

He looked at Elizabeth then. Her gaze was lowered as though she wished not to see the examination she had caused. She lifted her gaze, boldly looked into his. And then, with a brief though tender glance toward Giles, she lowered it again.

Jameson handed the warm damp cloth to Abigail. Covered her timid hand with his and pressed it to the coarse mat above Giles' cock. And Giles made not a sound, tensed then eased his stance. And Jameson went to him, standing at his side so he might look down to see both Abigail's hands and Giles' erection, though the latter had yet to arrive.

Jameson oiled his hands from the vial at his hip, then touched one slick palm to Giles' belly, the other to Giles' rump. "Her touch is gentle," he said low in Giles' ear. "She will prepare you for my blade." He slid the side of his hand into the crease between Giles' buttocks, letting the length of it brush over the tightness there. And then he brushed upward again so there would be no mistake for Giles to what came next. "Her hands small..." Jameson said, and angled his hand so his fingertip press the tight hole Giles sought to protect, his muscles clenched, nearly trapping Jameson's hand between them. "...and delicate," he said easing over the tension there, his oiled finger pressing ever so slightly, smoothing over Giles' anus as Abigail removed the cooled cloth and pressed another warm one to Giles' pubis. "Much smaller than mine... yet it is mine you will feel now. And you will not resist."

Giles trembled, a slight ripple of apprehension.

"Calm, Giles," Jameson said, his voice as tender as his touch, that touch pressing slightly still, then smoothing over Giles' tightness again, spreading the oils, softening the muscles, though only just. And then he reached down, brushing Abigail's hands away, and gripped Giles' drowsy cock in his hand, squeezing lightly prepared again for Giles' hiss.

The instant it quieted, the instant Giles exhaled and he accepted it, Jameson pierced the tightness of his anus, sliding his finger two knuckles within. Holding fast to Giles' cock. Not pushing further into his friend, only pulsing his probing finger, slowly. As slowly, as calmly and steadily as his hand pumped Giles' swelling cock. And then he stopped, let Giles calm his breaths. Jameson's own lodging in his throat as Giles' cock failed to respond well enough.

Be he marked, Jameson would spare him the gallows. Somehow, he would help him to escape. Though aiding a witch…

A harsh groan came from Giles and Jameson loosened his grip. Held Giles still, pressed forward, easing his finger in further. Watching Giles struggle beneath the blind, his hands clasped, fingers flexing and stretching above Jameson's wrist as he probed further, then withdrew and eased back in again. His pressure slight though consistent, in and out again.

Few were the accused who did not rouse to such a touch. Though many resisted, it overpowered, stirred them as only the forbidden would. Yet Giles… true to the man he was, of honor and duty, did not resist, did not shy from the touch but allowed it. His muscles softening, welcoming. And Jameson twisted his wrist, angled it downward so his finger might reach that tender spot which sent men to the cusp of release. Gently he stroked it and Giles' fear-filled tension faded to pleasure Giles seemed eager to know.

Jameson withdrew his finger again, pressed two forward against the tightness there, sensing his friend's desire, yet seeing no proof of it even with this touch sure to rouse.

He held Giles' cock firm in his hand, the need to arouse him much greater now, not only for ease of the blade so fine hairs might be removed, but for proof of Giles' ability. Tension took hold of his friend, trapping Jameson's fingers barely a knuckle within.

"Breathe..." He drew out the whispered word, rushing it no more than he rushed past the tightness again, his two fingers steady, sure, neither forcing nor relenting. "Push," he said, "as if to force me out..." The moment Giles complied, Jameson slid further inside, pressing, onward, until both fit deep to the web. And then he held still. His fingers buried in Giles' pulsing heat.

Impaled behind and gripped in front, Giles' trembled. His head back, his mouth agape, breaths cutting through him harsh and hard. Yet his cock lay silent and unmoved.

"Only the witch cannot feel Giles," Jameson said, his voice a gush of breath. "You feel..." He pulsed his fingertips within his friend, and there was no mistaking the sensations scoring through him. Yet proof be needed, proof Giles' senses had not been stolen, his soul still unmarked, his body untouched by the beast.

"Tell me," Jameson said, slowly easing his fingers from Giles until he withdrew them completely, his need to find the proof to save his friend. "Tell me you feel..."

"Aye..." The word sounded painful to say. "I feel," he said his head rocking side to side, "...but...I cannot..."

Jameson loosened his hold on Giles' cock, stroked him gently, steadily. "Did you lay with Elizabeth, Giles. Or did you not?" Did his cock fulfill or deny such joining, or did their joining still his ability?

"She...is innocent."

"She has stolen your –"

"Nay…" Giles' every breath was pained, full of need, of want. Moist. Impassioned. Yet the rise of pleasure, the surge of blood, the pulse of desire did not result. "Nay…"

Elizabeth cried. Her soft whimpers pulsing on short ragged breaths.

He glanced at Abigail as she shifted, her fingers, laced, her brow low and worried as she held his gaze. Her eyes confused. Himself unwilling to declare his friend marked. Yet Giles still struggled for pleasure.

"Giles." His voice rasped from concern. "If you lay with her, and she be a witch —"

"I am not a witch!" She cried openly now.

Jameson looked at her then, saw the pain on her face, the desperation as she looked from him to Giles.

"He did not lay with me…" Tears changed the tone of her voice, stripping its pride, tightening it with anguish. "Please Giles…I beg you. Please tell him true!" Her fear lay as bare as she, yet he knew not the cause. Giles suffering? Or his lack of arousal, which did not bode well for him. Or for her.

Jameson went to the hearth, used hot water from the kettle there to wash the oils and Giles from his hands. Needing the moment to find his own strength, for to condemn his friend would be to condemn his own soul to an eternity of grief and doubt. He dried his hands over the flame. Turned to find Abigail comforting Elizabeth. Abigail's eyes, tear-filled, pleaded with his from across the room. He heard her unspoken words. They mirrored his. Help them. Stop this madness.

He cut his gaze from Abigail's, unable to do as she asked. As he wished. His own hand, patient and knowing, had saved many, while another would do as was done to Giles. Torture. Maim. Force the innocent to admit guilt...

Yet Giles had said he did not make such admissions. The young boy he was endured great pain and humiliation. Stripped. Bound. Blinded by pain...

Blinded.

Jameson went to Giles. The blind over his eyes hiding that which lay in this room, not that which lay in his memory. Pains of the past. Of a child, a boy not quite a man...

Jameson took in the sight of that man. Proud. Brave. His body strong and tight. His manhood...

He eased the blind from his eyes and dropped it to the stool beside him. Giles blinked, his gaze on Jameson's. Steady. Concerned. Emotions Giles could not hide.

For years they shared secrets, as friends often do. Shared meals and fears and thoughts of this madness now stirring their village. And always, they two, shared truth. The eyes do not lie. And Giles' lay bare. Then, always, and now.

"Did you lay with her Giles?" Jameson asked, concern tightening his throat making his voice gruff.. "Did you spill your seed for Elizabeth?" He would await the answer, sure of it now, though it would pain Giles' to admit. For though Giles wished to save Elizabeth, this proof, which failed to appear would condemn her instead. "If it be as I believe," he said to his friend, "then you can prove neither her guilt nor innocence. Did you lay with her, Giles?"

"Nay." The admission came on a breath of despair.

"Yet you examined her."

"Aye, with my eyes and hands alone, and she responded…"

"You seek to protect her…"

"She is innocent."

Jameson stepped yet closer to Giles. His heart thundered like the frenzied march of anxious villagers as his understanding came yet clearer. "You came to be here, like this, to save her this same fate…"

"She endured more at the hands of the crowd."

He clasped his hand to Giles' arm, guided him to stand before Elizabeth. Her tear-filled gaze on Giles'. Abigail's shifting from one man to the other.

"You touched her flesh…" Jameson said. "You awakened her and brought her pleasure…" He looked at Giles. His proud friend. Honorable. Fearful. "Yet you did not succumb."

"Nay."

"Why?"

Giles inhaled as to fuel words but spoke not one.

Jameson turned his friend to face him. "Why, Giles, would a man such as you, not succumb to her beauty?"

"In that way," Giles said with the slightest shake of his head, "I am no man at all."

Jameson looked at his friend, saw him only. The women, the testing implements, the villagers dismissed, as brutal clarity dawned as bright as this night's high moon. "'Twas not the witch who stole your manhood," he said in a whisper, and the pain of that truth cut deep. "'Twas your interrogators. All those years ago."

Giles' eyes grew moist. "Aye." His voice, rough.

A roiling wave of fury threatened Jameson's control. To torture a child, to torture the man he would become, to have no care for truth only pain that lasts to death…

Jameson would end this madness if he could, would tell all there be no witches, only fear and imaginings. They would not believe, and in his stead would be another examiner. One, perhaps, as cruel as that for Giles.

He cupped his hand to the back of Giles' neck and leaned into him, touching his forehead to his friend's. Their gazes still locked. "You are more man than many. This I assure you. This, I will prove."

Giles closed his eyes, pressed them tight, and Jameson released him. Took him to the wall beside Elizabeth, not trusting himself to remain there longer, not while fury at others pulsed through his veins. "You will not touch her," he said, though he did not recognize his own voice, "until she is proven unmarked." He locked a shackle to Giles' wrist and turned away, needing to be free of this place.

He went into the hall, the door to his chamber sealed tight between him and the others.

He would see Mercy now. Let Giles recover. He took a step down the hall, then stopped, unable, unwilling to go further. Unable to trust his own hand in that moment, for injustices carried out were not merely by others, but by himself as well.

The Watchman

Chapter Four

Abigail rushed into the hall, still frightened for Elizabeth and pained for Giles, but worried more for Jameson. His calm, his ability to soothe and see past lies, warmed her heart. Yet the concern in his voice and anger in his eyes as he discovered Giles' truths drew her concern, for she feared where his thoughts had gone. She feared, too, for Mercy as Jameson's anger was a frightening thing.

He stood in the hall, at the edge of darkness where candlelight did not reach. His back was to her, his fists at his hips, as though lost in his own imaginings.

She went to him, her slippers silent on the wooden planks. Her shadow loomed before her, doubled her size, rising up on Jameson as though to embrace him.

"Good Sir?" She thought to touch him, but withdrew. Unsure what need he had. For his posture, though rigid, seemed to shudder. "Your fear for Giles lingers," she said, feeling the heat of Jameson's concern as it pulsed around him.

He did not face her, merely tipped his head away without response.

She placed herself in his view. Ached to help him calm. "You bear his pain with more burden than he," she said, well understanding, for she saw that anguish on his face when he saw Giles's scars, and felt the tremor of his hand as he touched them.

Jameson looked at her then, truly, as though seeking more.

She touched him. A hand gentle against his arm. It was warm beneath her palm. Solid. His physical strength tempered only by his kind heart. "You heard his cries," she said, "the cries of his youth. As though you were there, at that time. Did you not?"

He closed his eyes and when he would have pulled away, she drew him back. Understanding his pain, wishing he might understand hers.

"You felt the lash upon his back as though it sliced your own flesh." She wished not to add to his suffering with her own but to make him see, so others might know that to feel these things, to know the pains of others was no sign of evil, of witchcraft or magic. 'Twas but proof of a heart that loved. That cared. As she had cared. As she had loved. As she had confessed to a friend who did not understand. A friend who betrayed her and called her *witch*.

"These many years later," she said, "he has healed." She hoped truth, though unable to soothe her accusers, might soothe Jameson.

Instead, his eyes grew darker. His anger resurfaced. "They crippled the man he would be." His voice was not his own. Still sure. Still commanding. Yet strained, nearly strangled. "And others, I am certain, for many are those burdened by such tortures, or by confessions they should not have made."

"Good Sir…Jameson…" She flattened both hands to his chest. "You soothe that burden as you touch and arouse. Your words, your desire to prove innocence… 'tis not like that of the others."

"Nay. 'Tis not. And so 'tis a fate I cannot escape. Should I try, another would take my place and I would have no say in their care of the accused, thus condemning more to such tortures."

She shook her head slowly, aching for words to comfort him. "You are fair and just. Should you seek an end to this…Jameson…the villagers…they will hear you."

"An end." He cupped her cheek in his hand, so hot, then brushed his fingertips along her jaw, so light they tickled, drew her toward him. "Abigail…" The smallest smile touched his lips then faded. He dropped his hand from her and turned away, putting several paces between them. "For as long as fear lingers in the hearts of those beyond the gates…" He waved his hand toward the manor doors at the candlelit end of the hall, beyond which the villagers seethed, "…in the hearts of those sated only by another's blood…there be no end."

"Tell them of Giles," she said, her skirts rustling around her as she swept toward him. "Tell them of his bravery. Of the shame and terror we have all endured. Jameson…tell them there be no cause for more of this." Her plea was a mere whisper. "They will hear you…you above all."

Fury lit his eyes. "Or they will accuse me as well!" He strode toward her then, his step determined, and she drew back. "Who then would take my place, Abigail?" He drew closer still, towered above her, not stopping even as she stepped back further. "Would it be Samuel? A man who sees evil even in beauty?"

Her back touched the wall and still he came closer.

"He who inhales fear from those near him?" He leaned closer still, his nearness sending chills through her. And then he tipped his head closer to her, angled it toward her neck and inhaled, deep and long, as though breathing her in. "Fear such as that which fills your heart? They would smell it."

He pulled back, locked his gaze on hers. "Men, as he, devour fear then spew it back, ten-fold, in words covetous and cunning." He lifted his large hands as though to capture her face between them. She flinched, fearful of his touch when such anger darkened his eyes. And then he shifted, nailed his fists to the wall at either side of her head, looked down at her as she looked up at him.

"Those men, Abigail." he said, his voice low and dangerous, "they seek not to prove innocence of others, but of themselves, some excellence."

Could he not see his own excellence? His own power and cunning? She lifted her own trembling hands, pressed them to his waist, crawled them up to his chest, and felt his heat, the hard pounding of his heart, the strength of him as she pushed to ease him from her. He did not budge.

"Those men breathe fear while you would soothe it," she said, and disappointment shined clear in his eyes, as though he sought a different truth. "The others...they would hear you...Jameson...I believe this true." She could not ease him back so tried to pull him closer, grasping at the linen of his doublet, holding it tight in her fists. "You can end this." She held tighter when he made to pull away. Her fists trembling against him. "Begin this night. Release them. Giles and

Elizabeth. They are innocent. Say it, and all will know it be so."

"Only Giles' innocence is known." He dropped his hands from the wall and clasped her wrists, held tight, pulled until she let go of him. He stood back, straightening himself as though in resolve. "Elizabeth…must still be examined."

Elizabeth. So prideful. So sure innocence would spare her. "She has suffered most this night," she said, unable to stop the shudder that rocked her as visions of Elizabeth came to her. Stripped bare by the villagers, bound and probed by their greedy hands…it was torture of another kind. One without scars to see or touch. Defiled so, Elizabeth's defiance had grown but stronger. "She will not submit."

He nodded slowly. "You see it now," he said. "There be no end. Thirst, in the village, for a witch's blood shall indeed be quenched…at dawn, when Elizabeth hangs."

"Nay, Jameson…" She reached for him, grasped at nothing as he turned away. "Please!"

He strode ahead, into the darkness and she ran after him.

"Good Sir! Her fate…it shall be only as you permit…" He alone held the power to save her or see her hang. He would not condemn her…it could not be. "It is in your hands…" Her step faltered in the darkened hall, his steady boot-step echoed. Her heart ached, her chest tight from dread and her own fury at his refusal to see reason, much as the villagers whose hunger for blood he cursed. "'Tis you who inhale fear!"

He did not cease nor reply.

Though her breaths came hard, she held her chin high. "What will you do…Good Sir?" Her grief, her anger, thickened her own voice. Hardened her resolve. "Condemn her to prove your own excellence?"

He stopped then, did not face her, but stood rigid.

Rage at the injustice filled her. "Perhaps 'tis you who are not sated! You, who thirst..." She silenced herself too late. Yet the pain of his inaction...

He turned ever so slowly.

Her words should not have been spoken...nay not even thought. Untruths they were, each word, and all. "Jameson..." She inched toward him, had meant only to soothe, yet added further weight to his worry. "'Twas my anger...misplaced..."

There was fury in his stiff posture, menace in his sudden and quick step.

"Forgive..." She scurried backward like small prey from a hound.

He snatched at her, his grip tight on her arms, and pushed her back to the wall, held her there. "You dare question my honor?"

"Nay!" she cried, knowing she had. "'Twas in fear I spoke...you are unlike the others...Good Sir...your hand, most fair —"

He crushed her lips with his. Kissing her. Hurting her. His mouth unforgiving, unrelenting. Silencing her words, stealing her breath.

It was neither the kiss of passion, nor of need or want. She knew his heat. Had felt his desires, had been brought to trembling weakness by his expert touch. She would gladly take all that from him again. This...it was fear, anger and defeat.

He gripped her hair, held fast. The other hand pressed to her back, crushing her to him, closer, harder, his mouth forcing hers open, and she allowed it, accepted him in. Breathed with him, inhaled him, tasted him. Clutched at him. She wanted him, his pain, this pain her words created. Wanted as much to comfort him as to be the one he chose to do so.

His hands slid over her body, snatching at her. And then he clutched her hands in his, tugged them above her head, one of his swallowing both of her wrists, holding them there.

She whimpered, unable to move, to touch him. Soothe him.

At once, he pulled away, releasing her. "Abigail." His gaze lingered on hers for the longest moment. Hard and troubled. His breaths harsh. His brows gathered as one. "My anger is not for you," he said standing further back from her. "I should not have made it so."

He turned away and she reached for him, drew him back, wished to lift all burden from him...though it was only he who had the strength to bear the weight of it. "Jameson...I am unharmed."

"These hands," he said, lifting them, "nearly condemned you earlier. "

"But they did not—fair they be."

"These eyes saw the mark upon your breast...fooled they were. Be that fair?"

"They saw truth and saved me—"

"And Giles, if there had been cause to test him further...would I see guilt or a tortured heart?"

"Jameson—" She shook her head slowly, hurting for him.

"Elizabeth...her pride, her defiance...signs of evil, all. Her body, beautiful even now as she stands bound. Be she marked by the beast or filthy hands alone? Be it her beauty that shines doubt upon her guilt?"

"Those who seek evil see it even in beauty, you said this—"

"Is what once proved guilt now a trick to the eye? Can all who are accused indeed be evil...or might those who accuse be the evil ones?"

"Fatigue clouds your mind," she said softly. "Concern for the boy of Giles' past hurts your heart...that is why doubt lingers."

"No more this night." He closed his eyes, only briefly. Inhaled. "There will be no doubt." He straightened then. To his full height, looking down at her, resolve shining fierce in his eyes. "You would be wise to remain here as I tend Mercy," he said. "For with her, my hand will not be stayed."

He brushed past her and she hurried after him. Frightened of the darkened hall, a space where she had not entered so deeply before. And then, he opened a door and she hurried to follow him into the second chamber. The chamber where Mercy remained. Bound. Eager for his touch, a punishing touch he would too willingly bestow.

Though lit only by candles and hearth, the room shown brighter than the blackened hall, illuminating Mercy as she hung there still, her arms above and bound, her head dipped forward as though she slept.

Jameson stormed over to her. Slapped his hand to her rump. The crack of flesh against flesh sudden and loud.

Mercy shrieked, danced on her toes as far as her shackles would allow.

He strode behind her, ever at her back as she turned to and fro to see him. "You drowse, Mercy," he said, "when you should consider your fate."

"I drowse," she said on a harsh moist sigh, "for my thoughts do bore me."

He spanked her again, the sound of his palm against her rump painful and biting. Though Mercy's breath rushed from her, he showed no sympathy, striking her again and again and again. Making her squeal and squirm.

Abigail thought to run to him, to stay his hand, but his warning rang so clear in her mind she remained rooted at the door. And his hand came down several more times, each strike as hard as the first. And then they stopped and he stood there, watching her quiver. The crackle from the hearth and her heavy breaths the only sounds in the quiet room.

Then he cupped his hand to the spot he had punished. Did not pinch nor squeeze even as a soft coo came from her. He curved his palm to her flesh, his fingers slightly splayed. His large hand covering much of one cheek despite the generous swell of her.

"And what of this night, Mercy?" he asked softly, smoothing small circles over the spot, steadily, absently.

Mercy arched her back, lifting her rump toward his hand, not hiding from this touch, but seeking more of it. And he moved with her, stood back to look down at her, gliding his hand over her gently, without the aggression of moments ago, as though absorbing the heat of her, soothing her. His touch…his gaze…so intent. So sinfully reverent.

He had stroked Abigail with the same light touch as this. His fingertips grazing over her. Flesh to flesh. Warming her. Stirring her even with that slight touch as he examined her for the mark. As he awakened her. Made her yearn for desire she had not yet known…

"Have you no thought for what you must endure?" He stroked Mercy's hip, her thigh…lower to the back of her knee, then lower and lower still, until he reached her ankles and released the shackles there.

"What must I endure...please tell me," Mercy said. "After this time, locked alone in this chamber, I am unsure." Her legs free, she turned as he rose.

He moved with her, ever at her back, circling with her, as the ropes held her wrists high above and she shifted to find him.

The sight of them, in this dance, took Abigail's breath. Even naked and bound so uncomfortably, Mercy moved with grace. Her body bare and lovely. Her breasts so full, lifted as they were with her arms above. Her rump, tinted now, pink, from having been thrashed so forcefully. She spoke with lust not fear. And he, Jameson, so broad, so regal even through this long dark night, stood tall and sure behind her no matter how she turned, his hands on her waist, his gaze on her alone, though with beauty such as Mercy's, Abigail could expect him to look nowhere else.

"You will endure pleasure Mercy," he said and the sudden change of his voice, the low tone of it, from deep in his chest created a flutter within Abigail's bosom.

She knew that tone, it had rumbled beneath her palms as they pressed to his chest, stirred her hair when he stood close to her, so close, she felt the moist heat of his breath against her ear...

"Pleasure," he said, "perhaps beyond that which you have known." With anger aside, or masked, for the moment, the tender timbre of his voice remained.

With both hands gripped to her hips, he stopped Mercy's movements. They faced Abigail as she stood by the door.

"You will seek it..." he said to Mercy. "And you will suffer for it." His hands rode up into the delicate curve of her waist, traveled higher, to her breasts, and Abigail could not look away.

He cupped them. Held them a long moment and Abigail's flesh warmed as though the heat of his touch reached her.

"The witch cannot feel," he said, kneading Mercy's breasts as would a lover. Gently. Leisurely. "And as such, her lust cannot be sated." He smoothed his thumbs over her nipples in light steady strokes.

As though his touch were against Abigail's own flesh, her own breasts ached, craved. Swelled. And then a sigh, quiet and yearning, escaped her as he plucked Mercy's nipples so they stood firm.

She looked at him, startled to find his gaze on her as he touched Mercy. Watching. Studying. Knowing her secret desires. Desires he had roused in her...before, when he examined her...and now...as he rolled Mercy's nipples between his fingers.

"The bite of the clamps," he said lowering his gaze from Abigail to Mercy, "do you feel it still?"

Mercy tipped her head forward as to see his hands upon her. "Aye." Her response was low, a breath.

"Your screams filled my chambers upon their removal."

She glanced at Abigail, lowered her eyes again. "I felt great pain."

"It pleased me." He pinched Mercy's nipples, drew a small whimper from her, then lifted her full breasts, pulling them up by the tender nubs. The sudden aggression drew Abigail's gasp with Mercy's. "Your cries proved this part of you unmarked," he said and jostled her breasts as they hung from his fingertips, his hungry gaze steady upon them, as though taking yet more pleasure from Mercy's torment.

She bore it bravely, released but another small whimper, though whether in misery or bliss, Abigail did not know.

And then a muffled cry came from her, one she seemed reluctant to utter. She tipped her head back to rest against Jameson's shoulder and that cry turned into a low moan.

"This pleases you," he said, lowering her breasts, yet showing no mercy to her nipples as he still pinched and milked them between his long fingers. "It arouses you...despite the pain."

She rocked her head side to side against his shoulder as though lost in the pleasure of his touch. "Aye," she said on a sigh, hard and satisfied.

"'Tis lust, Mercy," he whispered by her ear. "Insatiable."

She trembled as though chilled, aroused by his breath upon her.

He released one nipple and slowly, slowly, smoothed his hand down over her belly, his fingers, his palm flattened against her. "'Tis that which brings you here this night...to stand accused." He reached his hand down further, to her shaved mound.

Abigail's throat tightened, her own need rising as he roused Mercy. And then his long thick fingers reached Mercy's core, burrowed deeply between her swollen lips.

Mercy's moan came low and long, the sound as stirring as the sight of her lost in pleasure while in his arms.

Jameson's arms.

Her body swayed there, her hips rolled sensuously. And then she tipped them toward his hand, buried there, and he pinched her nipple with the other until his fingers paled, the cruel touch seeming to punish her pleasure even as he roused it. He lifted her breast again and she stilled. Fell silent. Her belly clenching. Her breaths halted.

Moisture gathered at Abigail's own core. Moisture. Need. She should not feel such desires...for Mercy, though she craved, clearly suffered as well.

"'Tis this," Jameson said, bringing his fingers from Mercy's core to her mouth, three of them, glistening with her juices. "This passion which cannot be sated." He pushed them inside her mouth, though force was not required for Mercy did not resist but opened to them. Wide. Letting him stroke in and out. Deeply. Deeper until it seemed she should choke. "This passion which you must control."

He withdrew from her completely, without warning, unhanding her and putting distance between them, distance Abigail knew brought a chill to Mercy's flesh.

Mercy lowered her head, as when they had first come upon her, and her hair fell in thick waves over her face. Her breaths heaving from her, her legs pressed tight to each other as though to subdue desire.

Jameson reached for the bolt in the wall behind him and with a flick of his wrist, the intricate knots in the ropes came loose. "You are here, Mercy, accused...for 'tis feared your heat be fueled by darkness."

A small hiccup of a sound came from her as tension eased on her arms and she slowly lowered them. "'Tis not so."

"Nay?" He held her again, from behind, his hands on her shoulders, her neck.

"Nay...for what of the men who so freely visit," she said softly, "who readily spill their seed for me..."

His fingers pressed into her flesh, working the muscles there. Surely, they ached in ways they had never before. "Perhaps 'tis darkness which draws them to your charms."

His large hands stroked her arms, whether still soothing her or feeling for the devil's mark, Abigail did not know. She had searched Mercy's lovely flesh with her own hands. Had examined her fully as Jameson examined the others. And as she smoothed oils over Mercy's body, and probed her with her own oiled fingers as Jameson had taught her, she aroused only herself, not Mercy, thus failing her. Yet Abigail knew there lay no mark upon Mercy's flesh, save one small blemish upon her neck. Should Jameson find that now, she would tell him Hannah, Mercy's sister, bore it as well. Surely, the same mark upon twins was no sign of evil.

"Perhaps, 'tis within them, not I, where darkness resides." Mercy sighed and seemed to melt there in front of Jameson. Greedily basking in his heat and power. "But test me, as you will." She breathed contentedly, relaxed her shoulders as he soothed them. All but reclined her lush nakedness against him, and he made no move to stop her. "I am here to prove my innocence, not the guilt of others."

His arms came around her, his hands grasped her breasts, squeezed until she whimpered. "You would be well to remember that, Mercy, for 'tis guilt not innocence which deflects."

"Aye," she said with a sigh.

Abigail had not moved from the door and still could not. Unsure what to do, not wishing to watch more of this, yet unable to turn away. Perhaps she should have heeded Jameson's warning and not followed him into this chamber.

She closed her eyes against the sight of them. Of Jameson subduing Mercy's aches. And Mercy, smiling, sighing, aware Jameson's attentions would be complete and thorough.

Abigail ached for him to prove Mercy's innocence, now, in these very moments. Wished he would arouse her fully, no longer tease but let her find release, then permit her to be clothed and freed. Away from here. Away from him.

But there would be no doubt. He had said so himself, and so he would not cease, but work to arouse Mercy in ways Abigail could but imagine. Ways, it was known, Mercy craved. Ways Jameson, Abigail feared, knew too well.

She cupped a hand to her closed eyes, tried to block the view further. Still saw it in her mind, while in her ears, Mercy's words echoed.

As I writhe beneath his touch you will instead wish for proof of my guilt.

Though how guilt could be rendered on one so rich with passion, she could not know. 'Twas passion that proved innocence, yet passion which brought Mercy to be accused...thus bared for Jameson's hands.

The sound of Mercy's smile tinged her sighs and floated on musk-filled air. Abigail looked at her again, unable to resist. Mercy's smiling gaze remained fixed on hers. Teasing her. Taunting her. Knowing her secret yearnings. Challenging her.

Jameson's gaze lingered on her as well. "Whether before you or behind you, Abigail, you will shut the door."

For a moment, she thought to run the other way, to leave the manor and all sins and sorrows behind. She was innocent. Proven so by his hand. A hand patient. Determined. Relentless…

Yet the others…Giles…Elizabeth…

Even Mercy…

Slowly Abigail turned and closed the door before her. Unable to leave this place until all judgments were made.

She faced them again, stood taller against the amusement in Mercy's eyes. Glanced at Jameson, as he took the clamps from the floor behind Mercy, hoping he was not displeased by her decision to remain.

He looked at her then, a long moment in silence, as though permitting her time to reconsider. She stood taller beneath his steady gaze, determined more than before to remain. With him. And with Mercy.

"Come," he said, his tone softer than she expected.

Without haste, she went to him, her gaze on his, not Mercy's, though Mercy watched her every step, Abigail knew without seeing.

He handed her the clamps, his warm fingers brushing her palm, sending prickling tingles through her. And she held them there, her hands open in front of her, unsure of his intent.

"The ache, Mercy," he said, gently sweeping Mercy's hair from her shoulders to lie against her back, "in your arms, does it trouble you still?"

She breathed a smile. "Nay, your tender ministerings eased the ache most thoroughly."

He leaned into her then. "That is good," he said. "Then you will raise them once again and settle your hands behind your head."

She did as commanded and though she cringed in clear discomfort, she made not a sound.

"Clasp them," he said in a soft whisper. He waited, watched as she shifted then moved to stand before her. The three of them in an incomplete circle.

He took one of the clamps from Abigail, touched its edge to Mercy's breast, just a slight brush against her, like the sharpened edge of a blade scratching. Lower. To her nipple. Mercy gasped at the contact, whether in apprehension or pain was unclear.

"Nay, Mercy?" A mocking tone rang in Jameson's voice, as though a dare to Mercy. "Have you here a tender spot?" He stroked the iron over her nipple again, back and forth, following the rise and fall of her breast as she breathed heavily, the pressure of the clamp pushing her tight pebbled nub this way and that. "Perhaps a spot so tender arouses still," he said. "Perhaps too much to control."

Mercy's eyes shined with a rare flicker of concern, then warmed as he latched his hand to her breast and kneaded it softly.

Abigail did not warm at the touch as she watched, her concern too great, for it told her he readied Mercy for the bite of the clamps yet again.

"You would have done well, Mercy," he said, "to refuse these tests by my hand, and to accept those of the villagers, your lust so great."

"'Tis only one hand I seek..." she said, and her gaze skated longingly over him, even with this threat of pain.

"A knowing hand?"

"Aye," she breathed.

"There is but one hand strong enough for the witch," he said, his hand still holding her breast, the clamp still flicking her nipple. "One hand alone to slake the witch's ardor...be it that hand you seek? The hand of the beast?"

"Nay." It was a whispered vow of assertion.

Abigail believed. Yet Jameson seemed to question still.

Mercy's gaze flicked to Abigail, and in it Abigail saw Mercy's concern. Before she could speak for her, Jameson clamped Mercy's nipple.

She cried out, clearly unprepared.

Instantly, he removed the clamp. "You will look at me and me alone," he said rubbing his hand over her breast, her nipple, as if to soothe the ache, this punishment not meant to be too severe.

Mercy breathed through it, the slightest smile curving her lips, passion lazing her eyes.

He clasped her chin in his hand, seemed to study her eyes. "What do you seek here this night, Mercy?"

"To show you proof of my innocence."

"Do you believe it will be proved?" He released her and took a step back. "For I am unsure."

"It is truth."

"Your time in the pillory," he said, "'twas but a taste of what you shall now endure...here...where no one will see or dare stay my hand." He tipped his head the slightest toward Abigail.

Her flesh tingled, certain he warned her as well as Mercy.

"No matter your sighs..." he said in a whisper that hummed from his chest, "...nor your screams." He stroked his free hand over Mercy's hip, then cupped her core, and she breathed a smile. It faded as he lifted his wetted hand to her mouth, brushed his glistening fingers over her lips. "You are able to resist the pull of lust?"

"I..."

He reached between her legs again, his fingers clearly probing her, tugging her nether lips, his hand seeming to know, on its own, where to go, how to touch and stir her, for stir she did. Her belly tensing, her hips rolling.

"Consider your words carefully, Mercy," he said, "for I believe you are nearer release than you will admit."

Abigail opened her mouth to speak, to beg him to grant Mercy release now, to send her from this place, from Jameson himself. Yet no words came forth, silenced was she by her own shameful lust. Lust roused by the mere sight of Mercy's pleasure. Pleasure much greater now than in all the time Abigail had spent with her earlier.

She swallowed, noisily eager to see Mercy's torment ended. "Good Sir…with pleasure so clear as Mercy's," she said, "surely she is unmarked."

He did not look at her but at Mercy as his fingers still roused her. "'Tis not merely pleasure I seek, Abigail, for Mercy's pleasure is known." He eased his hand from her core, gripped it to her hip. "'Tis control of it I wish to see now." He lifted his other hand, held the clamp before Mercy's eyes, then brushed it over her chin, along her jaw. "Breathe deeply, Mercy," he said in a whisper, "for we begin."

She did as told, her chest, her breasts, rising with each slow deep breath. Her hands still clasped behind her head, elbows out to the side.

He stood closer to her, his free hand smoothing over her back, grasping her hair and slowly coiling it about his wrist, his fist. "You ache for this, do you not?"

Her breaths came quicker, harder as she gazed up at him, their faces so close their lips could touch, their tongues could dance, their breaths could tussle as lovers in lust. Abigail would hold her own breath could she catch it as she awaited Mercy's words.

They came in a whisper. "It would be a gift from your hand, this pleasure…"

He held her a moment, looked only at her, her eyes, and she at his, as though only they two existed. "Widen your stance," he said, and his tender tone tamed his meaning.

Mercy shifted, spreading her feet wide apart.

"I will awaken you further," he said softly, calmly, winding her hair tighter, forcing her head back as he trailed the clamp down the length of her throat. "I will see need rise yet higher in your eyes. I wish to smell it with my every breath." He brushed it between her breasts, then lower. Slowly, precisely. "I will feel it," he said, "see it, and know you fight to control it…"

Her belly quivered as he trailed the clamp lower still. Leaving no doubt of his intention.

"And you will, Mercy…for to do so will prove your innocence. To do so will save your life." He eased back from her slightly, did not look away.

To Abigail's surprise, Mercy shifted, widening her stance yet further.

The smallest smile touched Jameson's lips then faded, as though he and Mercy shared some unspoken tease.

He released his hold on her hair, brushed his hand over her back, her hip, his gaze never leaving hers, speaking to her without words. And then he cupped her core again, stroked her with his fingers, and the slickness of her need sounded the same as an eager wet mouth against flesh. He pulled his hand from her, and then plunged his fingers back into her, making her legs, her entire being tremble. He offered no support, and though Abigail would offer her own she barely stood herself, the sight as stirring for her as troubling.

Yet Mercy bore it all, her legs spread wide, her hands clasped behind her head, her breasts lifted and displayed...And then he grabbed one swollen nether lip between two fingers and locked the clamp onto it. He stood back, not holding her as she swayed, her mouth open, only moist breaths gushing from her, a compelling mix of distress and desire upon her face.

Abigail's own response came in a rush of breath, and slowly Jameson looked at her, his darkened gaze one of lust the same as Mercy's. Abigail could not deny him that, for her own need pulsed deep within her as well.

"Abigail..." He lowered his gaze to her fist, the remaining clamp held tight within it.

She opened her hand, held the final clamp out to him.

He took it, and turned back to Mercy. And then he pinched her other nether lip, and clamped the second iron to it.

Mercy whimpered, trembled there before him, the clamps dangling from her, the weight of them tugging her nether lips downward. Her brows had gathered in a pitiful bunch, her breaths grew rapid, yet she released neither cry nor complaint.

"Walk," he said. "To me." He backed away from her, slowly, taking smooth easy steps backward toward the center of the darkened room.

Mercy adjusted her stance. The heavy clamps swayed and clanked as she took a first awkward step. And then, with a slow deep mesmerizing breath, her grace returned and she all but floated to Jameson, seeming unhindered by the large irons hanging between her legs.

Abigail followed, her own step, though unhindered, faltered as a shameful desire to learn what would befall Mercy next assailed her. It distracted her with each step she took until she saw iron rings mounted to the floor behind Jameson. What purpose they held, she knew not, yet feared.

Jameson held up a hand, stopping Mercy with Abigail beside her. They remained there, facing the darkened corner of the room until he stood back and waved a hand toward the irons on the floor. "On your knees."

Gone was the stirring tone of his voice, the low rumble he had used just a moment prior. This command was deliberate. Bold. His gaze steady upon Mercy. Impatient.

Abigail raised a hand to urge Mercy forward, certain resistance would cause her greater suffering than her compliance.

She moved without aid. Stood in front of Jameson, her feet between two of the irons. And then she lowered herself slowly, unsteadily to her knees, her hands still clasped behind her head.

Jameson snatched at them, roughly. Lowered them. Then he pushed her forward until her forearms were flat to the floor, her rump high in the air. He circled her then, his step heavy, purposeful, stopping before the rings in front of her.

"Reach, Mercy," he said.

She dared a look back at Abigail, a fleeting though potent glance, then did as he urged, stretching forward until her hands slid through the rings by his feet. And then she touched her forehead to the ground.

As he watched her, he furrowed his brow, shook his head slowly, though how Mercy displeased him in that moment, Abigail did not know for she had followed his command.

He eased down to his haunches before Mercy. Touched a hand to her hair, brushing it in a deceptively gentle caress. "Do your ears fail you, Mercy?"

"Nay."

He grabbed her hair in his fist, pulling her head up until she looked up at him. He seemed not to hear her startled cry. "Repeat my command," he said.

She was silent and Abigail held her breath.

Jameson waited, his gaze solid on Mercy. "Be you so fatigued you have forgotten?"

"Nay…"

"Shall I rouse you, Mercy? Perhaps a bucketful from the frigid well shall remind you?"

"Nay…reach," she said. "You bid me reach."

"And?"

"Naught else."

"Yet you rest your head."

"In deference to you, nothing more."

He snorted a small laugh. Released his hold on her hair, smoothing it as she held her head up, looking at him.

"Abigail," he said, and tightened the rings about Mercy's wrists. "There is a large cloth pouch upon the table." He looked at her then angled his head toward the door between the chambers. "Bring it to me." He stood then, slowly, watching her, his gaze, unreadable though reading her, as though knowing how great was her wish to end this now.

She cut her gaze from his, started toward the door between chambers then turned back at the sound of his boot step, loud and determined it was in the quiet space.

He faded into the darkened corner, then one by one, lit candles upon the wall and within a candelabra there, illuminating that part of the chamber, bringing it to life in all its shocking and frightening detail.

Mercy breathed a sudden harsh breath. Abigail's breath was lost.

There were more iron rings. They were mounted at random levels on the wall and upon the floor. Several more hung from the ceiling. He lit more candles then turned, capturing Abigail's gaze, seeming to question her. To seek her thoughts though she dared not speak them. She looked past him where leather straps hung from iron hooks. Some straps solid, some slit into thin tails. A wooden spade hung there as well, its handle short, like a washing beetle. And a yoke, bulky and solid, though much smaller than one would need for an ox. Chains, thick and thin, long and short. And poles of varied heights, some with shackles at either end, some standing bolted upon a block, as though waiting for something to be mounted upon them.

There was an iron claw, the same horrendous tool she spied within the chest in the other chamber. And more tools. Branding irons, weights, ropes, a substance like tar in a large jar, some candles unused…

"Abigail." His tone held clear warning.

With no voice to answer, she turned for the chamber where Giles and Elizabeth remained bound. She entered, her eyes lowered, unable to look at them, wishing they might not see the color of fear and need and confusion as it heated her face. Though in that room, she smelled their lust. The lust of many, the eager need to prove innocence. The breaths filled with want, with desire, with growing passions…

Silent now, yet lingering.

They gazed at her, Giles and Elizabeth, questioning. She did not see, did not look, but knew.

Focused on the pouch, she went to the table, and retrieved it, cared not what it contained, turned with it, not speaking. Hearing a long release of breath, like a sign of frustration. It was Elizabeth. Though just a sigh, it rang with her voice.

Not glancing their way, Abigail went back to Jameson, closing the door securely between the chambers.

The Watchman

Chapter Five

Giles had caused pain for Elizabeth when it was his wish to spare her. She stirred him. Awakened that which had been buried deep within him, that which was unknown to him but on the most rare occasion.

"Elizabeth."

She stood just out of reach, naked as he. The two of them alone. Silent. She, bound by one leg. He, bound by the opposite arm.

She cried only, an occasional tear and sniffle. She did not speak nor look his way. Her head down. Her hair the color of fired-bricks, luminous in the firelight. It fell forward, shielding her face in a lush curtain of soft tangled curls. Curls that had dripped from his hands when he held them high, exposing her long neck and bare back to the villagers. They had converged upon her at that time, as he had permitted. She could not resist for he had bound her arms high above her as required, so they might see all of her. Touch all of her. And they did with an eagerness not unlike that which he had seen before. Their greedy hands snatched at her flesh, probed her, marked her...then called that mark the devil's.

Not even then did she cry but submit to the cruel pleasure of those hands, showing clear proof of her innocence while shame and fear ravaged her heart. Fear of her fate. A fate he wished to alter. A fate now certain by his own failure. Failure to make them see her response to their touch. Failure to respond, himself, to Jameson's.

Lest she plead with him, with Jameson, and submit herself again—not to the villagers, nay, but to Jameson's hand—she would see the gallows at dawn.

Concern softened her posture, yet he feared she would not relent, for her pride, though impressive, was potent and damning.

"Look to me, Elizabeth."

She shook her head slowly. "I had asked, Giles, why you would comfort a witch..." She turned to him and he recalled the question from when he had brought her to the forest, bound her and tried to warm her. Soothe her.

"I did not see a witch then," he said. "Nor do I see one now." Shackled by one wrist, he reached his unbound hand toward her, wanting to cup her soft cheek, to whisk away the stain of her tears, but the distance between them was too great.

The slightest smile, bittersweet, twitched upon her lips then faded. "That is what I am," she said.

Her gaze, so sad, lowered to his hand as he dropped it, unsure was he of her meaning.

"It is what they see," she said. "Out there, where they cower together. And within these walls. To all except you, I am a witch. And it matters none for I will be one of many."

He would not permit her to succumb to such thoughts. Would fight for her if she thought not to fight for herself. "You dishonor yourself, Elizabeth."

"Dishonor?" She laughed and it was a short pained sound. "Giles...I defended my honor when I refused to submit to him, our governor, and his vile touch. Yet...I permitted the same for you. You are most honorable while I--"

"You are innocent," he said. "Are you not?"

Her pride surged, it was clear by the defiant lift of her chin. "Aye."

"Then it is not you, but innocence I defend. Would you take that from me?"

Her proud stance sagged. "I saw your pain as he touched you," she said. "I felt it Giles. And I did not stop it." She touched her hand to her cheek, flicked away an errant tear. "If it were innocence you sought, and you found that in me, then it was I you defended. For that, I am grateful. For that, I am no longer innocent."

"That is your own logic," he said. "Of sense to no one else." It was a lie, for he understood and felt the shame of his own guilt, though her effort to defend herself was to be admired not shamed. "I witnessed the fire in your eyes." In truth it was that fire that captured his heart, for fire so great, defiance so sure, was proof of a heart too proud to relent, and of a will broken only by the greatest effort. "You would defend yourself still," he said, "but this...fear, this madness...it is too strong."

"Stronger than I."

Frightened was she, yet calm. Clear of mind. Her will, unbroken. "You stand here now," he said, "brave as when you were bound in the forest...when I brought you there."

"'Twas your eyes. Your voice. Gentle. Kind. You gave me courage."

He could but shake his head. 'Twas her courage alone. Her wit and determination, for she had pleaded with him to examine her. To allow her to prove herself, there beneath his hand.

"You gave yourself to me, Elizabeth. You allowed my touch when you fought the others. Your need, your trust..." How could he admit the truth? That her beauty, exposed to him against her will, that her body sorely tested...stirred until it craved while her mind refused...her will bent until she submitted...It was shameful, but... "It awakened me, Elizabeth."

His words were crude for one so fair and ravaged, yet she did not cower from them but seemed eager to hear more.

He took heart. "'Twas not my desire to see an innocent suffer. 'Tis not our governor's desire..."

She waved a delicate hand as to silence him, her striking green eyes closed tight. The very mention of Jameson seeming to cause her pain.

"Though you do not believe...Elizabeth..." He waited until she opened her eyes and looked at him again. "He is a man with honor. His touch...is meant not for pain or grief but proof of innocence."

"It is meant to shame. How could you not see this?" She laughed and it was a tearful frustrated sound he wished to quiet, to soothe. "I saw him Giles, I saw his hands on the others. I saw the flush upon their flesh, the need in their eyes..."

"As was his wish."

"I saw his arousal as well," she said. "Beneath his breeches. Though he sought to hide it from us." She pressed a hand to her chest as to soothe herself. "Aye, 'tis pleasure he seeks…not merely for the accused but for himself as well."

"Elizabeth." The fire within her still churned. For that he was pleased. And concerned. "He is a man," he said, "surrounded by need and naked flesh." He let his gaze rake over her and though he had the view of her body for hours this night, and touched her soft smooth flesh, aroused her, felt her heat and succulent desires…he imagined her now as Jameson might. As another to please, another to awaken, to stir until there could be no doubt that innocence be hers. "It is true, his desire must be fulfilled, for his desire is to prove innocence. To do so, he must arouse all in his care, to have them submit in body and mind, to his words, his touch…to their own need. You cannot begrudge his pleasure from that."

She wiped at new tears and the remnants of old, seeming angered by the evidence of them. "And what of you, Giles?"

"I do not begrudge him that small pleasure, for that pleasure, unfulfilled, is no pleasure at all." He felt deflated, in heart, in hope. In body. Himself unfulfilled. His desire to prove her innocence a fool's plan. Only she had the power to prove herself.

"I submitted," he said, his gaze roaming her body, seeing, unseeing, wanting, needing. He looked away. "I submitted this night, to Jameson only, for I know his hand be fair. Though unyielding as well, 'tis never more than what the accused can bear. Yet…" He looked at her then, his gaze unwavering, needing her to know… "I felt fear, for there are few whose hands do not remind me of the past."

Jameson's touch had been strong. Firm. Yet somehow gentle, as though each caress was a vow not to harm. A whispered promise that pleasure alone would be had, and that fears…pain…from the past…need not surge. His friend knew, understood and cared. "He does not take pleasure from these examinations but hopes to give it."

"Yet he caused you pain, and fear. I saw it in your eyes. So brave, so frightened. He did not bring you pleasure."

"Nay…I could not—"

"Giles…why…how did you hope to defend our lives, if you…cannot…" She glanced toward his wilted cock, and he barely resisted the urge to cover himself. "Why?" she whispered, her gaze not mocking but gentle upon his.

"You stirred me, Elizabeth. When no one else could. There…in the forest, as I touched you and you yielded…" At her passion, her need and trust, he had felt the churn of true desire deep within his gut, the pangs of which shocked him in that moment. And then, with an insistence he had not known, that desire mounted, uncomfortably so, engorging him past pleasure toward pain, need. His own. For her. "I believed myself cured," he said. "By you…"

Her smile was small and fleeting, but lovely. "Did you not believe yourself bewitched?"

He was bewitched. By her beauty, her pride and her bravery. Yet as quick as he thought himself cured, disgust at his traitor body had quenched those stirrings, for her desperate fear should not have aroused him so. "Nay." Truth told, he wanted to touch her again now. Have her yield to him again. Yet their distance, as they were bound…it was painful. "I wished to save you, instead, I failed you…"

"Giles…" She shook her head, crinkled her delicate brow, her gaze searching his. "Why…did they torture you so?"

He would not speak of it. Not now when they should speak of her fate should she not seek mercy from Jameson. "'Twas another time," he said.

"It was in this time, not many years ago, in your youth. Who did you defend then Giles? Who was the innocent you sought to protect?"

"She was my own mother." Anger, terror and denial. He had felt all of that and more when they took her away. Himself, his brothers, running after the cart. Calling to her. Shouting over the creak of the wheels. Gasping in the choking dust. It seemed it barely settled and then he and his brothers were carted off as well. "She was made to witness cruelties against her sons. Myself and my brothers. And she confessed. Yet her screams of guilt, through tears and pleading, did not stay the interrogators' hands, for they wished her fate be sealed by all who knew her."

One word could have saved him. One word could have spared her the sight of his torture. Spared him the sight of her pain for him.

One word.

Witch.

Elizabeth stirred, sniffed and he looked at her, brought his thoughts back to this time, to see it was not his suffering that needed comforting now.

She blinked and new tears fell. "You did not succumb."

He shook his head slowly. "Too many innocents perished." He watched a tear roll slowly down to her jaw. It lingered there, though barely.

Slowly, she lifted her hand and wiped the tear away. "Your brothers?"

"They were younger than I, tender more than myself." His gaze remained on her hand as she pressed it to her throat. "My confession would seal her fate," he said, "as all she loved turned against her. I could not. But it did not matter. A witch, so accused, so confessed, was to be destroyed."

"Giles..."

He had suffered for her, his mother, and for all those struck by the accusations, all those misunderstood and wrongly charged. As Elizabeth. No more a witch than his own kin. Yet tongues wagged, and pride surged, sealing their fate.

"She was not unlike you," he said. "Her own defense sure and loud. She fought her accusers, fought her interrogators, and the brutal tortures continued, grew, until her own children be used against her." He lifted his gaze to hers, held it, hoped she would understand. "Only then did she submit. But then, Elizabeth, it was too late."

"You...stand on the side of accuser, Giles. As watchman. Yet you defend the accused. I do not understand."

An accuser he was not. Not now or ever. "I could not save her," he said. "I bore their abuse. I looked at her eyes, eyes wide in horror, as they flayed my flesh. It was because she struggled so, neither meek nor silent was she, and for this they punished us further. I seek to keep calm, to prevent the madness from mounting now as then. I can do little to sway decree but share my thoughts with the governor. As he is fair, he hears the voice of reason even when madness would have it silenced." Yet, now, after the crowd's insistence Elizabeth be marked, his voice alone would not be enough to spare her. Her own defiance had tied Jameson's hands, not permitting him to examine her, to prove her innocence. And as dawn grew nearer, the opportunity to do so dwindled to a mere crack in time.

"His words were true," she said, tears in her eyes yet again, "you are indeed more man than many."

Perhaps not all Jameson's words but deeds were true. "He is not as you see him, Elizabeth. I wish for you to know…"

"If I misjudged him," she said in a whisper, "then all was for naught…your struggles, here in this chamber….beneath his hand and Abigail's…if not for my poor choice, you would not have been brought here and tortured so."

Her words struck him like the fall of a whip. "This was not torture, Elizabeth. What you endured was not torture." He thought of his brothers, younger than he… "The binding of children, bending them so necks met ankles…the merciless bite of the whip…that is torture."

Torture was the sour smell of blood, the smell of his own now affixed to his memory. It was the laughter of his tormentors as their pleasure at his pain and fear bulged beneath their breeches. His own arousal had blossomed as well, adding much to their amusement. And only as years idled by did he know his body had awakened in response to the terror of it all.

He thought of the women, like Elizabeth. Accused. Shamed by their nakedness before all, aroused for the pleasure of the crowd, brought to levels of passion they had not known, for all to see, to hear and cheer. The pain of that was great, no doubt, but none such as that which true tortures begot. "Beneath Jameson's watch and determined hand, Elizabeth, there is, at least, hope."

"He is determined to prove your manhood."

"Aye." He thought then of Jameson's large hands against him. How each stroke of them brought new awakening. Small shocks like the stings of bees. Yet as the strokes continued, as Jameson's hands gripped and caressed and warmed, the stinging subsided, the fear of pain, though it lingered, masked by new sensations. Of promise. And he ached for it, Giles did. He sought the pleasure of his friend's patient touch. Though pleasure remained, as always, just out of reach. Neither Jameson's firm grip on his cock, nor his fingers probing behind, permitted need to flow. And despite the maddening tenderness of Jameson's strokes deep within him, forcing need, it fell again as his thoughts did stray. His desire to prove ability so great he failed to do so. Yet again.

He looked at Elizabeth. Thought, too, of Jameson's hands upon her. He had been rough with her. Cruel. For she did not seek it. His anger at her pride, his fear at her presumed guilt, turned Jameson's gentle hand to one of vengeance, determined to punish her for her resistance.

He knew his friend well and could speak to him again. Though his word alone would not be enough to sway his mind, Giles could easily show him how deeply Elizabeth's passions lay. Then, should she yield, he need only stand beside her to feel it. To know heat coiled deep within her. So deep as to be incompatible with the witch.

He would touch her himself should she again permit it. He would show Jameson how true her responses could be. He would touch all of her, with light caresses. Inhale her scent, delicate it was, yet rich with her need.

He ached as much to touch her as to feel her touch…her caress, her embrace, the warmth of her sweet breath against his chest. Her lips to his—those lips as ready to spit angry fire as mewl in notes of need. Her fingertips, her touch, against his scars...would they sting as well? He wished to know.

She stood so close to him now yet too far. And need swirled inside of him. Need to have her, to bring her pleasure. To free her.

She brushed her long hair from her shoulder, the riotous curls, as defiant as she, teasing her nipples as they slipped over her breasts to brush her shoulder then settle with several small bounces behind her. Her fingers lingered there at the delicate hollow between her shoulder and neck. He would bury his face there, breathe her in, bite the tender flesh, lave his tongue over the wound. Hold her. Allow her to hold him.

Her hand shifted and she smoothed the back of it against her jaw, her neck. Slowly, he lifted his gaze to hers.

She did not look away. "Giles..."

"Were it my hand against your throat now," he said surprised by the thickness of his own voice, "I would feather it over your breasts...unable to resist, I would be."

She brushed her hand downward as he spoke. Did as he said he would do, and he all but felt her soft flesh beneath his fingertips. "My hand would linger there," he said softly, not looking away from her hand against her breast, "with strokes light and barely there...just a hint of what would come..."

Her fingertips grazed the full swell of her breasts, slowly trailing over them, and her breaths, as his, grew longer. Slower.

"You would feel my hand, Elizabeth, upon your belly. Seeking, stirring as I felt your breaths on my face..."

She smoothed her free hand downward, over her belly as he said, then lower, her fingertips straying into the small patch of curls more riotous there than on her head.

"I would taste you," he said, wishing he could. "Touch you then lick the wet heat of you from my hand. I would bury my fingers deep inside of you..."

"I would welcome it, Giles, the thrust of your fingers."

The breathless tone of her voice, the lush desire within it, brought his gaze to her eyes. But she did not look up at him, instead her gaze strayed toward his cock, which stirred now beneath her attentions, though like a drowsy man at dawn. Hope roused it, tightening his belly as the hand on her breast caressed her nipple, plucked it as he would do with his fingers, his teeth.

"Face me as well you can," he said in a whisper, and she did, the chain at her ankle rustling against the floor. "Spread yourself for me." He waited eagerly as she shifted, her legs beautifully spread, her hands never ceasing their exploration of her body. "Do as I would, Elizabeth. As though your hand were mine." Her fingers burrowed between her swollen nether lips, parted them, and one disappeared inside of her slowly, a mere breath at a time. And his breath was lost. "Another," he said gripping his rousing cock. Thinking only of her pleasure, pleasure she now sought, did not fight. His hold on need fragile, timid still as she slid a second finger inside of her body, slowly easing both in further.

The chamber door opened and Abigail came through, her eyes averted as though she knew of their actions. Giles' cock throbbed, petulant now when he would have it hide. Elizabeth's shackles rattled as she shifted, her breaths, a moment ago soft and steady, now harsh in a frustrated sigh.

Abigail's face was flushed, though not in pleasure, for her brows were low as though in concern. She took a pouch Jameson had set on the table earlier when Mercy had screamed, and as quickly, Abigail left them, closing the door behind her.

Giles thought of Mercy, fearful for her and what she must now endure.

He gave his cock, sleeping now, one last squeeze, then turned to Elizabeth again. By not submitting to Jameson's hand, she would be spared Mercy's fate, but the fate that awaited her was final and one he would fight to disallow.

Slowly she smoothed her hands over her body once more. Though he craved to see her pleasure, he would permit it no further, for if she should choose to seek mercy from Jameson and should he grant it, then her pleasure, so close, would be sure and swift, thus sparing her much distress by Jameson's hand.

Her eyes, deep green now, like the forest, desire darkening them so, looked into his as though seeking direction. And then she cupped her breast, unaware his desire now was not to watch her pleasure herself, but to keep her roused and ready for Jameson.

"Stay your hand, Elizabeth."

Confusion flickered in her eyes.

He could not explain. Could not speak. He ached to see her pleasure, pleasure by her own hand, by her own choice...it would bring him pleasure as well, but cause much danger for her.

"Clasp your hands at your back," he said and she did.

Her breaths came hard, her chest, her heavenly breasts, aglow with the blushing heat of her passion. Heaving. Demanding to be held, caressed and laved.

He closed his eyes. Still saw her body. In his mind. Those eyes, stubborn and frightened. That hair, in which he would bury his face and inhale…her hands so delicate, so strong…how he wished to feel them upon him, her fingers wrapped around his shaft, coaxing it to life, her palm lifting his tightened sac until she roused him further and it lifted on its own. She had that power over him.

"You awaken me, Elizabeth," he said again for it surprised him still. "Not as would the witch, but a woman of great beauty… and greater mettle. To my last breath I would defend you."

Her eyes glistened as she gazed at him. "'Tis my honor to have stirred you, Giles, even in some small way," she said in a strained whisper. "And 'tis my honor to stand with you now…" She swallowed noisily, blinked and tears fell, "…no matter how this night might end."

He reached for her, knew the distance was too great yet sought the contact. And she reached as well until their fingertips met. A slight graze alone. He wished for more, would touch her as he had in the forest, hold her face in his hands, wipe all trace of her tears and taste her.

Yet this he would take. These few moments. This fragile touch.

Chapter Six

Jameson noted Mercy's slight distraction when Abigail headed toward the other chamber. It was with a mere tilt of her head and a furtive glance. He noted too, how Mercy breathed once Abigail closed the door between them. As though Mercy had found new air that roused her, new energy to power her desires.

He went to her, each step slow and sure until he stood before her bound wrists. "For what do you ache, Mercy?" he asked, his voice purposely low, a rumble in his chest. "Tell me."

Her neck strained as she raised her head to look at him, her gaze slowly skimming over him. Inch by inch. From his boots to his breeches where desire contorted itself in restraint... then on to his chest... his eyes.

"For your hand," she said. Her eyes held need, not shame nor fear, as they looked into his. Ever the seductress she was, with a natural curve to her lips and with eyes that heated and cooled, challenged and accepted.

She lowered her gaze, her head, and he permitted it in that moment. "A hand well-learned have you," she said, "both tame and torturous." She looked at him again, coyly, lifting her gaze only. Her dark lashes like a veil between them meant to tease. "I ache for what you would provide."

He squatted before her, and clasped her chin in his hand. "I will see your eyes well," he said.

She opened them fully, searching his.

"You will not look away from me."

She shook her head slowly.

He held her chin tighter, stopping the motion. "You will neither feign modesty," he said, his voice a low murmur, "nor endeavor to tempt me." He released his hold on her chin, gave her face a small slap, and noted her sigh. While others would flinch, shy from him in that moment, Mercy shuddered with desire.

He leaned closer to her, his mouth near hers. "It is not I who will be tested in this chamber, Mercy." He smoothed his hand gently over her cheek then slapped her a second time. Her sigh, her shudder. were nearly imperceptible, but there for him to see and hear.

"'Tis I who will test," he said in a whisper. "And I shall know whether your pleasures…your pain…be feigned."

"True they would be," she said, her gaze dropping to his mouth, "for pleasures feigned are efforts wasted."

He allowed himself a brief smile, certain Mercy, of all, wasted no efforts.

He turned from her, and went to the corner where various floggers hung from hooks on the wall. He chose one, a thin-tipped crop with which to begin.

The creak of the chamber door drew his attention and Abigail came through. Gently, as though to not disturb, she eased the door closed behind her, then turned his way.

He forced his gaze from her and went back to Mercy, noted how she lowered her head, as though the effort to keep it lifted had become too difficult. He would have her full attention upon him so he might gauge her responses properly.

"You will keep your head raised," he said, and then without warning, reached forward with the crop and landed a sharp swat against the side of her breast. He ignored her gasp, his attentions drawn to Abigail.

She stood as stone. Her lovely eyes, unblinking. Her lips, those lips he had crushed with his own while in the hall, just moments ago, parted slightly. Her confusion clear, for his handling of Mercy was unlike that of the others. Mercy, Abigail would learn, craved much more, and he would provide it all. Though he wished sweet Abigail would not stand witness, he wished as well to witness her responses to such arousals as he would administer.

"I will test you, Mercy..." he said, turning back to her. "...your breaths...your body." He feathered the tip of the crop across the back of her neck, crawled it over her flesh as though time cared not but to wait. Listened to her sigh and coo.

He made his way around her, his step unhurried, brushing the crop down her spine in a light caress from shoulders to rump.

"Your pleasure and need." He stopped behind her, stood between her bound ankles, then lowered himself to one knee. Her scent, her desire, oozed from her, stirring in its potency. "They belong to me."

With his free hand, he took hold of a clamp hanging from her nether lips. Ever so gently, he tugged on the clamp, a steady pull that stretched the flesh to which it clung. He let go, watched as her tender flesh bounced back even as the dangling clamp weighted it still.

Her body clenched. The muscles in her thighs, her rump, tightened as though soaking in the sensations.

"You will find release," he said and smoothed his palm over her rump, presented to him so beautifully, "...only should I permit it." He stroked his middle finger along her slit, so moist between her clamped labia. "Do you ache still..." he asked, "...for what my hand might provide?"

She ground her herself against his finger. "Aye."

He withdrew his hand, trailed his moistened finger down the length of her inner thigh then back up to the clamps once again. He cupped both in his palm. Lifted them. Jostled their weight against his hand, and then released them. They swung to and fro, holding tight even as she made sharp little sounds of surprise, even as she wriggled her hips in time to their swaying.

Their bite was firm. Perhaps too much so, for he wished not to numb her flesh, but to awaken it. Make her aware of that part of her with every moment that passed, every breath, so she might be roused yet higher. With one hand, he gripped both clamps and gave a slow steady pull to them, stretching her nether lips again.

"Be my hand tame?" he asked, using her own words. "Or torturous?"

She smiled; he heard it in her sigh. "Both," she said, "for there are pleasures to be had if only you see them as such."

He glanced at Abigail, pleased to see not a flicker of surprise pass over her eyes at Mercy's admission. Though he wondered if it had caused her thoughts to flitter elsewhere, as his. For had that truth, Mercy's truth, been so for Elizabeth as well, then perhaps the only marks upon Elizabeth's body would have been proof plain of her pleasure, accepted not fought.

"I assure you...Mercy... " He pulled the clamps more firmly, still steadily, gently. Not forcing them from her. Letting her feel the tug as they slipped from her flesh bit by bit. "...though you will see those pleasures, you will not taste them lest I say you may."

He pulled the clamps more firmly and her gentle sighs turned gruff, clearly aware was she of what came next.

The clamps came loose with a cold sharp snap, freeing her for the moment. He dropped them to the floor.

She did not move nor breathe, seeming to prepare herself for the hard pulsing ache they both knew would come.

He did not wait for it. Would deny attention to her response to it. Attention, she so craved.

He strode around her, stood where she would see him, yet did not face her, simply shifted the candelabra there instead, his back to her. All the while, hearing, not seeing, her writhe against her restraints in a dance meant to shake off the pain. And then she whimpered, the smallest sound. A sigh.

She calmed. Quieted.

He turned. Not to her but to Abigail. "Rest the pouch there upon the table," he said as she stood still at the door with it in her hands, "and come here. To me."

Her intent gaze on Mercy slowly shifted to him. He would hold that gaze, force it to his, not Mercy's, for Mercy's pleasure would be roused too much by such wonder upon her.

He went to Mercy's side, withdrew the vial of oil from the pouch upon his hip, and held it out to Abigail.

She hesitated a moment as she stood across from him at Mercy's other side. Then she took the vial from his hand, seemed to study it, to study him.

Unlike Mercy, Abigail had feared his touches when he had examined her. Yet, she did not resist, and he had found himself awakened as never before. Wanting her as no other. Needing to prove her innocence…innocence which should have never been questioned. Yet doubt and rage stirred all those beyond the manor. It billowed as the wind. Wayward. Careless. With no evidence to its beginning, no hint to its end.

He wished to end it this night, and declare innocence for all. Yet he knew not whether his words would still soothe, stirred as the villagers were. Roused beyond all he had known…fear blinding fairness.

"Good Sir?"

Gently he covered Abigail's hand with his. He would declare truth, whether dark or light, and all would hear. He would make certain so innocence might no longer suffer. He tipped her hand and the vial.

The oil fell in droplets onto Mercy's lower back. It lingered there, warming as he knew it would against her heated flesh.

He spread it over her with a light steady brush of the crop from where it had landed toward the dimples above her rump. Then he lifted the crop from her, and Abigail raised the vial again, letting another small bit of the oil fall.

Mercy writhed and sighed as it slid in a slow languid path down her spine from her hips to her shoulders. Abigail breathed a soft hum, the sound most arousing. She swallowed that sound as it faded, seeming surprised, ashamed of her response to Mercy's coo.

Jameson looked away, taming a smile, pleased as much by Abigail's arousal as by her discomfort. He strode around Mercy, and lightly, carefully brushed the crop where the oils still lay. Her body quivered with her every breath, with every pass of the crop against her. Over her back to the graceful swell of her hips, her waist, her breasts, full and hanging freely there.

His booted step was loud even to his own ears in that small quiet space. The light wisp of the leather against her, soft and soothing. His breaths, Abigail's, as steady as each stroke. The movement of the keeper fluid. The leather, slick now from the oil, gliding smoothly over Mercy's body like a moist and greedy tongue.

These touches, so light, would be pure torture for one who craved, one who welcomed a hand rough and unyielding. Yet Mercy sighed, glistened and writhed there in the firelight.

"You stir with these tender touches," he said softly, both pleased and concerned by the fact. "Yet it is a heavy hand you crave."

"It is your hand I crave," she said. "Most agreeable it is."

He moved behind her, laid the crop's thin staff long-ways beneath her rump where it curved to meet her thighs. "And your time in the pillory," he said, and slowly, with gentle pressure, sawed the staff over that sensitive spot, certain she recognized the feel of it, like the switch. Certain she knew the pain of a switch. Perhaps even sought that pain... "You found your time there agreeable as well?" She had been sentenced to a day in the stocks, though the hours there did not tame her ways, and the magistrates sentenced her a second time. Bared. Bound. Bent over in the center of town, her head and hands locked in place. The crowd taunting her, touching her. A most humbling occasion, though not once, even then, had he heard her cry out or plead for mercy.

"The villagers…" she said with a sigh, "…greedy were their touches. All for their own pleasure, and as such most disagreeable."

With a flick of his wrist, he snapped the crop to her rump, a sharp bite of leather against flesh. She squealed in surprise and he gentled his hand, brushed over the spot softly before striking again. Once. Twice. He did not pause at her whimpers, her writhing, but struck several more times upon the same spot. "Punishment, Mercy," he said, "is not meant to be agreeable."

He stopped then. Did not touch her. Did not soothe but let the sting linger so she might feel it well and deep.

He went to the table, set the crop down and opened the pouch Abigail had brought from the other chamber. A wealth of implements lay before him, though now, in this moment, he needed only one. He withdrew a small box. Five spars made of stone lay nestled within it. Various sizes from the slimmest to the most stout. For Mercy, who found pleasure in pain, he would use one of a more sizeable girth, though not, by far, the greatest.

He brought it to Abigail, glanced at the vial in her hand, and she drizzled its oil over the stone. He spread it well, then stopped for a moment, amused, as she added more.

He took the vial from her, set it into the pouch at his hip, then turned to Mercy. He did not look at her, merely strode past her, sure she would see the well-oiled stone he held so she might prepare herself for what would come.

He cupped his slickened hand to her rump, then lightly stroked her with the rounded tip of the stone. Sinking its fat eager end between her full cheeks, settling it there against her most secret spot, though not so secret for Mercy. He smoothed it over that tender hole, lightly, sweeping gentle circles over it, awakening the muscles there, preparing them. And then he pressed more firmly, a steady pressure mounting until the tension there softened, and her tight muscles permitted the very tip inside.

With a sigh she arched her back as though seeking more of it.

He held it still, forcing the sensations to linger, to grow. And then he eased it further inside of her, his effort so light as to make her crave. To make her feel every brush of it within her.

"You will take all I give, Mercy," he said, feeling the stone shift in his hand as her muscles clenched around it, seeming to hold it in place. He eased the pressure, willing to move slowly, yet unwilling to stop. "And you will hold it within." He would take her as high as he could, let her linger in that place where passion stood just out of reach, a breath away, until he need only say the word for it to consume her.

He pressed on, fed it into her slowly, the stone flaring wider toward the middle, smooth and rounded. He added more oil at its widest part, letting it drip onto her and pool where the stone and her body joined. Then he eased it further inside of her, stretching her bit by bit. Her moans, her sighs, were gruff, pained and needy. Her buttocks clenched.

He eased the pressure. "Breathe," he said, and waited for her to calm. "Accept it all, Mercy…take every inch." He started again, pushing gently, a constant force against the muscles which tightened upon the stone, seeming as much to expel it as to submit to it and permit it inside. Further stretching her, slipping now easily since the fattest part lay firmly within her, and then on until only the flattened base remained. A wide disk it was, pressed against her, holding her supple cheeks apart where it sat.

He pressed his thumb to it, to be certain she had accepted it all. Then he smoothed both hands over her rump, the oils on them making her flesh shimmer. Bringing sighs from her as her body adjusted to the cold, hard intrusion.

He released the irons at her ankles, then. Gently rubbed the tender flesh there. "Stand now," he said, and moved to release the irons at her wrists, rubbed them the same.

He helped her to her feet and she rose slowly, stiffly. "Clasp your hands at your back," he said and when she did, he beckoned her forward with the crook of his finger. Forcing her to walk toward him. To struggle with and against the sensations of the stone wedged so deeply inside of her.

Desire built in her eyes, showed her need rising. But a witch, so stirred, would have need for more. A greater touch, a harsher hand. Unable to control herself, the witch would be. Ever seeking release, for it would be found only at the pleasure of the most evil one of all. Not by a mere man, no matter how experienced his hand.

He stepped back again and she advanced further, slowly, her hands still clasped at her back, her breasts thrust toward him, her long supple legs shimmering in the firelight.

She reached him again and he remained where he was. She took another step, stood so close her nipples brushed his doublet. Eager points, they were. Hard, dark. Still sore from the clamps, he was certain. He wished to test them, to pinch them again, clamp them and see how well she withstood the sensations. Her needs, so great, too great…

He did not ease back from her, did not touch her. His desire instead to rouse her to the brink then let her manage the fall of it, control it, and prove herself able.

Slowly he lifted a hand, cupped it to her neck, then tipped her chin up with his thumb. "I wish you to feel it well, Mercy." He touched his other hand to her full soft hip and leaned closer to her, crushed her lush breasts to his chest. Whispered softly into her ear. "I wish to know how it rouses you, teases you…pains you."

"It pains me most terribly," she said and he believed her words, "for it makes me crave…"

He drew back from her then, just enough to still feel her heat. "You will suffer that craving," he said, "until I say it may be satisfied." He stood aside and the smallest of smiles flickered upon her lips as she looked at the pillory behind him.

He pulled the pin from the eyebolt then lifted the pillory's hinged top, exposing the grooves for her neck and wrists.

"Your pleasure is known to many, Mercy," he said and gestured toward it, inviting her to place herself, neck and wrists, within it. "Your need so great you render men unable."

"Pleasure well spent, is slow to return," she said, her voice a whisper.

She settled her wrists into the smaller grooves, and he pressed his hand to her back, guiding her down so she might place her neck into the larger curve.

He set the top into place and locked it with the pin. "The men whose wives were denied," he said going to stand by her head, brushing her hair back as it fell over her face, "they were spent, by you?"

"Aye…."she said on a harsh, heavy breath, "they were."

He snatched her hair in his fist, bent low so his gaze met hers, certain her flippancy was a lure meant to rouse him as he sought to rouse her, yet rouse him it did. "All of them?"

"Many," she said, and he tightened his grip on her hair, pulled. She heaved a sigh and Abigail smothered a gasp. "Some…have wives, so cold…," she said, "it is they who render their husbands unable." The smallest smile brightened her eyes. "Not I."

"You smile coyly," he said, his face before hers, "when it is humble you should be. When 'tis your own lust that sends you here, you should seek not to flaunt it." He studied her eyes. Those eyes that seduced, that displayed every lustful thought within her. Compelling others to think the same. To want. To need. "Or is it pride you feel, not lust, for taking the seed of so many men." He pulled her hair more firmly, awaiting her response.

Her breaths came steady and hard, her neck straining, locked in place as it was, her throat bobbing. "I do not take," she said, her gaze heavy yet fixed on his. "I receive."

He released his hold on her hair, let it fall into her face. No longer wishing to see those eyes, eyes that tempted without shame. Like those of the witch. "And well you shall receive now…"

He snatched the crop from the table, then stood behind her again. He wasted no time, having spent much preparing her already. He would bring her to the brink and deny her release.

Feet firmly planted, he slapped the keeper to her rump several times in quick succession, not warming her, not warning her, his hand not harsh yet firm.

She cried out with each crack of it against her, writhed as if to hide from the blows as much to find them.

He continued the strikes, five without pause, then a gentle smoothing of the keeper against her, and then ten more at a pace steady and firm, each following the roll of her squirming. And on he went, his hand tender then harsh until her flesh turned a sweet shade of pink, and her cries and gasps cut through her as one, the sounds most harsh and primal.

He struck lower, swept the leather beneath her cheeks, at her thighs. Back and forth, he slapped it over her, the placement of each strike directed where the prior one landed until the flesh there glowed as pink as her sex.

Her cries turned to harsh breaths. Grunts, nothing more.

He pressed the crop flat to her flesh then, firm pressure only, holding it there. "I would hear of your pleasure, Mercy, as you suffer for it." To emphasize the point, he drew back and clapped the crop firmly against her again.

She cried out as he wished, a shout of lustful surprise which drove him onward. Most pleased was he by her pain, for the witch, prideful and vain, would not display it so.

He moved on to another spot, lower on her supple thighs. Looked from the reddening flesh there to Abigail as she soothed Mercy with gentle strokes and soft words.

Abigail's lovely face contorted with concern as she stood before Mercy. Yet Mercy's cries were no longer of pain alone. Nay. Wanton pleas they were, for she sought yet more.

And more he would provide until she could no longer cry, no longer writhe, her need and fatigue so great. He would have it consume her very being until she would either plead for mercy so he might grant her release...or confess Satan's role in her passions.

He smoothed the crop over Mercy's reddened thighs and cheeks. Several steady light strokes against her. Then nothing for two breaths. Three.

With his free hand, he cupped her core. So slick was she, his fingertip slid into her quim without effort. He probed her heat, met no resistance and pushed on, filling her until his finger could go no further. Slowly, he withdrew, then eased two fingers inside, her body accommodating them with ease. He pulsed them there, deep within her, followed the sway of her body as she bucked against his hand. Pressed further, felt her muscles tense around him as she whimpered and moaned.

It was not enough. He would have more. He would have her scent filling the room, her cries of need teasing Giles and Elizabeth in the chamber beside them. Her body, heated by her own desire, glowing in the firelight, the candlelight. And her breaths, gasps of need only, no voice, no logic, no attempts at seduction. Only Mercy, wanting. Knowing only that which her body craved.

He withdrew from her heat, her hips rolling, tempting him to fill her again. And he did, plunging into her fully, withdrawing and plunging into her again and again until her sighs and her gasps became one. Then he withdrew completely. Permitted her a moment of writhing, then cracked the crop to her rump, welcoming the piercing sound of her yelp.

He rubbed his fingers together, spreading her juices over them. "I see you drip, Mercy," he said and smoothed his hand over her rump. Tugged the spar from her a mere bit, then pushed it into her again.

She trembled, her whole body shivered, and she breathed hard pitiful breaths.

"Yet I would see need pour from you." He stood at her side then, a hand tender against her back near her shoulder, curving below to cup a breast. "I would see need so sure, so near..." He kneaded her breast gently. Roughly. Its fullness overflowing from his hand, the creamy flesh so light against him. "...yet so far."

He plucked at her nipple, pinched it, pulled gently yet steadily until she ground out a moan. "Many shy from my touch," he said. "Yet you do not."

"Your touch..." she breathed the words, "it is not so harsh as some I have known."

He strode around her, stopped in front of her. Tapped the leather keeper to her chin, tilting her head so he might see her face, her eyes. Darker they were now, heavy. "And you have known many." He caressed her cheek with the crop, gave a light tap to it, then to the other.

"Aye," she said, and there was no humor in the admission now. It was quiet. Whispered. Anticipating.

With a nod, he moved to stand at her other side. Her breast, too long neglected by his hand, in clear view, its fullness irresistible.

"I would know your pleasure," he said, "and your pain. I seek both, Mercy. True and complete."

He slapped the crop against the side of her breast. Relished the sound of her cry, pained yet lust-filled it was. He struck again and again, her breast rocking from the impact. And he continued the strikes, more forceful now. Slap upon slap of the crop to the side of her breast, then striking upward against her nipple, slapping in time to her whimpers, her gasps. Each strike firm, quick. No break between.

Her moans grew in volume, the wood of the pillory creaking as she writhed within it, seeming then to hide from each strike as well as she could.

"Do not stir so," he said, "but accept this pain, welcome it. Show it to me complete, as proof of your innocence." Eager was he to hear her plea for mercy as he continued. Yet all he heard was the snap of the crop against her flesh, her delicate feet stomping, her gruff breaths…his…

With her flesh now vividly blushed, he eased the strikes, giving her a brief moment to breathe fully.

Abigail seemed to breathe with her…as though she felt the strikes herself and had held her breath until this moment.

He watched Abigail a few seconds more, noticed the flush upon her cheek, the way her eyes avoided his. And then he turned to Mercy again. Her lustful moans, her gyrations, were all proof of her mounting need.

He would hear more of her cries now, ached to know they were from a touch not so extreme, for a witch could bear more pain than a mere mortal. Even one so roused by pain as Mercy.

He moved behind her, struck the crop to her hips, first one than the other. And then her rump. The harsh smack of the leather hitting its mark, loud and satisfying, nearly as much as her harsh sighs, growing harsher. Though lustful, they were not pleas for mercy…pleas he most wished to hear.

And so he continued, his strikes faster, harder, giving her what she craved until a brilliant red splotch grew bright upon her rump. He stood back further, flicked his wrist upward, clapping the wicked tip against the underside of her rump, the move lifting her fleshy cheeks, making them jiggle and clench, the lick of the leather lulling. Even her voice, muffled at times, hoarse at others, soothed as though all was right. As though this heavy touch, this pain, was all she sought.

"Good Sir…" Abigail stood beside him, gripping his arm, an attempt to stay his hand.

He glanced down at her small hand on him, waited until she removed it, then went to the wall and hung the crop there, needing to push Mercy further, to get her to the point of breathless abandon. The point where guilt or innocence could no longer be questioned.

Paddles hung before him. Leather. Wood. Some slim and long, some short and stout. He chose a shorter one. Wooden. A paddle perfect for Abigail's hand. The impact of it concentrated, for her hand against Mercy would be more delicate than his.

He went back to Abigail, held the paddle out to her, patiently waiting for her to reach for it. Thoughts and questions swirled in her eyes as she hesitated.

"You will continue," he said to her, his gaze meant to cut through her shock, and command her compliance. Though Mercy gained pleasure by his hand, she would gain only frustration from Abigail's, of that he was certain. "Do as I did, Abigail."

She did not move.

He gripped her arm, turned her so she stood with her back against him, not permitting her time to consider as he covered her hand with his. Together they struck the fleshiest part of Mercy, the thud of wood against flesh most satisfying.

Mercy's low, hungry growl more so.

Wanting to hear it again, to push Mercy yet further, to surprise her, he held Abigail more firmly. His arm looped about her waist, pressing her softness against him, stirring him even as he sought to stir Mercy.

He lowered his head, his lips near Abigail's ear. "Again," he said softly, still holding her to him, but gentling his grip on her hand, granting her control of the swing.

Her hand was not harsh, yet she shuddered as though pained, while Mercy merely rolled her hips.

"Again," he said by Abigail's ear.

She obliged, then twisted to see him, her gaze questioning.

He nodded his approval, impressed was he. "Again," he said. "Steady, lest you grow fatigued." He stood back, granting her space even as he ached to press her to him again.

Abigail's brows gathered as one as she swung the paddle and held it against Mercy, the thud abrupt but soft.

"Smooth it over the spot then strike again," he said not wishing to see wounds upon Mercy, no matter her thirst for pain.

Abigail did as told, soothing Mercy as though wishing to raze the effects of her strike.

"Again, Abigail," he said, "do not pause."

She continued, weakly, though not from fatigue but concern. It shined clear on her face. Her innocence, her compassion, pleasing him now as before.

Yet, true compassion for Mercy required another touch, a touch elsewhere upon her while Abigail's touch, so tender, only teased.

He went back to where the floggers hung, and grabbed a pair of thick, leather gloves from the shelf beneath them. He slid the gloves onto his hands stretching and flexing his fingers until the leather fitted him just so. He turned then, went to a spot well beyond Mercy's view, the rhythmic thud of Abigail's paddling seeming to bounce off the walls as he moved. Then, from high on the wall, he eased a fresh branch of nettles from its hook. When wielded just so against naked flesh, nettles stung the same as embers still aglow. The burn of the plant harmless, though lingering. A fright for some as it grew. A thrill to those such as Mercy.

The leaves rustled as he shifted the light branch. Holding it in his grip like a paddle, he went to Mercy.

She sighed, and it was a small shuddering sound of discomfort. Her delicate brows gathered. The small furrow between them, a most telling sign.

"A fine harvest," he said, stroking a gloved hand gently over the leaves, careful to neither wound the prickly hairs upon them nor pierce his glove with them. "...cut for this purpose alone." He drew closer to her. "To test the witch." He plucked a leaf from the branch, held it before her eyes. "How cunning, this trick from nature," he said, turning it front and back so she might see the spindly fur upon it. "These hairs, so fine, appear most fragile."

He turned the leaf again, most carefully, not seeking to break the brittle hairs before their time. "Yet their bite is much like the sting of thickets, is it not Mercy? Their burn as from fire."

She tipped her face away from it, her breaths heavy, lips parted, voice silent. Her body jerking forward with each strike of Abigail's paddle. Her gaze fixed on the single leaf until he dropped it to the floor.

"She bears it well," he said, "does she not, Abigail?" He did not wait for her to respond. "Perhaps too well." He shifted to stand at Mercy's side, then held the nettle branch beneath her, between her breasts and the pillory's frame. "Strike harder, Abigail. A solid five for which Mercy will offer gratitude."

"Aye." Her response was weak.

"It is for her benefit," he said. "Strike harder. Five, hard laid on."

"Aye... Good Sir."

The strike hit its mark, jostling Mercy, her breasts bumping the tender leaves. He held it there, the stinging hairs abrading her flesh.

Her gasp was sudden and full, though she did not cry out.

"With gratitude, Abigail," she said, her words released in a rush, as though forced on a breath through gritted teeth. "Please. Another."

The second blow came, and with it a wail from Mercy, not from the paddle but from the nettles. The burn from the second strike atop the first, undeniable. Jameson knew it well. The effect from the juices in the stiff hairs, though immediate, would quickly grow to an almost unbearable burn. Yet she would bear it with pleasure as was her way. It would linger, seeming to sear the flesh, then slowly, ever so slowly, it would begin to fade.

"With gratitude?" He reminded her, shifting the branch to her back, holding it above her.

She breathed hard through her delicate nose, the air sounding thick and difficult to inhale, exhale. The scorching feel of the leaves clearly building to a place beyond pain.

"Aye," she said finally, and dread thickened the whispered response. Dread and longing. "With gratitude…Abigail. Please…another."

The paddle struck again and with the lightest touch, Jameson swept the branch across Mercy's lower back. Tiny red bumps appeared in its wake. She hissed, a long stiff sound, and he swept it over her again, then waited for her to catch her breath, to bear the pain as well she could. To respond with gratitude.

She did not, and he stood beside Abigail, then flicked the branch to Mercy's sore, reddened buttocks.

She screamed, a gruff sound ground from deep in her chest. Her breaths sharp and cutting, her feet stomping. Her hips, those full fleshy hips writhing beautifully before them.

"Please…" Her voice held a tremble. He waited. Held the stalk at his side. Hoped for her plea of mercy. A plea to show she could bear no more… unlike the witch.

"With gratitude," she said, then. "Please…another."

They continued their game until the strikes totaled five, and Mercy had felt the burn of all of the leaves. Her cries and whimpers grew to shrieks barely controlled. Her flesh grew to an angry red, both from the paddle and leaves, yet no plea for mercy came from her lips.

He tossed the stalk to the side, its stingers exhausted, then lightly scraped the stitched tip of his gloved fingers over her lower back, her rump, like fingernails against wounded flesh.

She trembled, breathed as though even that effort pained her, withdrew as well she could from his touch, but did not cry out. He waited. Patient. Eager to know whether she wished for them to cease all they did, or, like the witch, to accept yet more with ease.

He went to Abigail, her concerned gaze on his, the pain of the paddle clearly greater for her than for Mercy.

Abigail made to speak, and he silenced her with a shake of his head. He would show her the results of her attentions so he might ease her worried brow.

He cupped a hand to Mercy's core, welcomed her cry of surprise, let it fade, then plunged two gloved fingers within the slickness he knew would be there. He withdrew, turned to Abigail, sweet Abigail, and raised his gloved hand so she might see Mercy's juices glistening upon the leather.

She nodded slowly, then stole a glance at where his own arousal thickened and pulsed boldly beneath his breeches. A response he could not deny, torturous it was at times, as pleasures denied so often were. A lovely shade of blush grew upon Abigail's face, high upon her cheeks, though she did not look away.

With a knowing smile, he turned back to Mercy, still writhing there, and slid his fingers gently into her again. Probing deeply. Then deeper still. Then, with no rush at all, he eased back, bit by bit, noting how her muscles gripped him, as to trap him within.

He thrust into her again, held still, letting her have all he could give.

Her body clenched around him, and he withdrew the same, slowly. So slowly she would feel every smooth and rough spot of leather, wetted now with her need, need that scented the room with lust unfulfilled.

Her hips rolled, her back arched as he withdrew completely. She sought more and he would provide it, if only to tease, to tempt, to raise her need higher.

He dabbled his fingertips over her swollen nether lips, then pressed the flat of one between them, along the full length of her slit, nestling it there, teasingly, barely grazing her eager nub.

He held still, let her shift her hips and writhe against him, pleasuring herself there upon his hand. He permitted it, wished to drive her mad with need, to watch her thrash about with desire…desire he would not yet see quenched, but would have her control…

Shifting his hand, he plunged into her again. Teased the flat of his thumb over her perineum, pressed it to the spar wedged deep in her anus, pulsed against the base of it even as she ground against him. Her breaths hastened, her writhing a most wondrous sight. Abandoned lust, such a beautiful thing, seen by too many as evil…

Her body tensed, tightened yet more around his fingers as though release were near.

He withdrew. Heard her anguished cry of want, and Abigail's rush of breath. Felt the strength of them deep in his own stiff loins.

He moved to stand before Mercy, showed her the lust upon his glove. Touched it to her mouth, brushing it over her lips, leaving her glistening juices behind.

She licked at the wetness, nibbled her full bottom lip, suckled, seeming to savor her own flavor.

He watched every flick of her tongue, every languid blink of her eyes. "You are a greedy witch."

"Nay," she said on a breath. "I am not a witch."

He removed his gloves, and tossed them to the floor beside the nettles. "How will you prove this to me, Mercy, if your lust flows so readily? Insatiable it is…you cannot deny it." He touched a finger to her chin, lifted her head so she might look at him. Her hair stuck to her face, and he smoothed a lock of it from her eyes. They were lazy now, as though fatigue warred with yearning. And moist they were.

"What do you feel? You will tell me..." He leaned closer, whispered to her. "Do you crave release, can you not bear to wait any longer...or do you wish for more. Of my hand. Of the crop. Pain. Pleasure. Whatever I choose...?" He drew back. "How greedy be your lust? How patient?"

She breathed a weak quivering breath. "I am as you wish me to be."

'Twas innocent he wished her to be.

He brushed her damp hair from her cheek and from her neck, exposed the same slight mark borne upon her flesh as on her twin. A mark others, fearful of Mercy's lust, would deem the devil's own whether she be declared innocent or guilty.

He removed the pin from the lock, and lifted the hinged top of the pillory. "How do I wish you to be?"

"Burning," she breathed, "like fire." Slowly she rose, as though it pained her to do so.

He lowered the top, went to her as she stood behind it. "You burn, Mercy, for the most wicked of hands."

He wrapped an arm about her waist, held her against him and eased the stone from her anus. Slowly, so slowly her body seemed to draw it back inside. But on he pulled, her breaths panting from her, sighs sweet and dreamlike. And then it popped free, and he dropped it to the floor, held her more firmly as she swayed. Kept her in his arms until she stood well on her own, then slowly eased his hold on her.

Her eyes drifted shut and he steadied her.

"Your wicked hand..." Her eyes remained closed, her voice a low murmur, almost as though she slept. "...is most bewitching."

"Tis not I who bewitches, Mercy." He walked around her. Ran his hand over the small welts from the crop and paddle upon her hip, her rump. Swept it gently over her lower back, the lightest touch against the flesh stung by the nettles. Not halting his step until he stood before her again.

"Do you yet crave?" He captured her heavy gaze. Held it. Curled one hand to her hip, the other to the nettled flesh of her breast. Watched pain flicker in her eyes as the heat from her wounded flesh warmed even his own hand.

She tensed, hissed a breath as her eyes closed again.

He leaned closer to her, wisped his thumb in slow circles over her pebbled nipple, making it stand yet firmer. "Are you so eager," he said, keeping his voice as gentle as his touch, "you would receive more of my wicked hand?"

Her breaths were soft, warm. "Aye."

He whispered to her. "I will see your eyes."

They fluttered open until her gaze rested on his.

"Always in this chamber," he said, "you will keep yourself open to me. Your eyes. Your sex." He slid his hand from the luscious curve of her hip to her sleek thigh, grazing over the front of it. "Widen your stance." He skimmed his hand upward along her inner thigh, pressing there to part her legs further. "And lift your chin."

She shifted, her movements less graceful than earlier. Her heated body brushed his, yet he remained there, a mere breath before her. His gaze unwavering. Promising. Daring.

Her eyes lowered to his as she tipped her head back, their gazes broken only by her languid blink. Her breaths turning shallow and uneven, as though she hovered in a dreamlike state.

"Abigail," he said softly, without turning from Mercy. "Retrieve the pouch."

He cupped his hand to her core. His fingers grazing her moist heat, dipping into her welcoming folds, sliding fully into her pulsing sheath.

A breath, hard and moist, rushed from her in that instant. Her body tensed, her gaze fixed on his.

Pleased was he by the need upon her face. Need barely controlled.

He took his hand from her, and grasped four small steel clamps from the pouch Abigail held before him. "And now, Mercy," he said. "Your needs shall mount yet higher." Without warning her, without preparing her in any way, he clasped her nether lips, pinched them. Pulled on one and snapped a single clamp upon it.

Before her gasp could fade, he snapped a second clamp to the same lip. Flicked it with his finger. Gently tugged. Assured it held well. Then he clamped the remaining irons to the other side until all four, two on each side, hung from her moist swollen lips, lips still tender from the bite of the larger clamps.

"You will hold your pleasure well, Mercy," he said and withdrew a tall thick collar from the pouch, a light steel chain hanging from the back of it. "You will endure until I say otherwise."

He wrapped the leather around her neck, forcing her chin higher, letting the chain drape down to the small of her back where it would ripple against her nettled flesh with her every shuddering breath. He buckled the collar snugly, watched her eyes the whole time. The concern, the excitement flaring within them.

"Unlike the witch, you can feel." He took two cuffs from the pouch, fitted them to her small wrists. A forged ring and two shorter chains, thin yet strong, attached to each. "Your lust clear." Her body shimmered there from the oils, and her own sheen of desire. "Yet I will know it be from nature, not the beast, so extreme you cannot contain it."

He cupped his hands to her shoulders, stroked the length of her arms to her hands, then drew them forward, and secured the chains from one cuff to the clamps on that side.

"It is now that I will know where your allegiance lies, Mercy." He attached the chains from her other wrist to the remaining clamps, then eased her arms a bit to the sides. The gentle tug of the chains pulled on the clamps, spreading her nether lips ever so slightly. "Lovely."

He released her arms, stood back, admired the lush beauty of the dark leather against her pale flesh.

She did not move. Seemed to dare not.

"Abigail..." He took the vial of oil from its pouch on his hip, poured a small amount into his hand, his gaze never leaving Mercy's. "Secure Mercy's hands at her back."

Understanding widened Mercy's eyes yet she did not cower, did not shudder in despair nor fear.

Abigail stood behind her showing the concern Mercy herself should feel.

He drew closer to Mercy. "You know my hand well," he said. And, too, she would welcome the blissful agony he would now bestow upon her. "You crave it still..."

Abigail hesitated. Did not speak, yet he heard her question clear. "Tight, at her back, Abigail," he said without turning from Mercy. "Then to the chain hanging down."

She did as told, and the delicious sigh she released as Mercy whimpered, stirred him, hardened his cock to an almost painful state.

The chain from her collar to her wrists forced her head back, her chest out.

Mercy shifted, bent her elbows, thus raising her arms behind her. It eased the pull on her neck, made her breasts less of a target. Though, with her arms raised, the chains on her cuffs peeled her labia wider, making her core yet more vulnerable.

A new sense of pleasure filled him as another wave of understanding bloomed on Mercy's face. He surprised her. Made her breaths quicken, her body shiver. Responses no witch would permit.

He stood closer to her, spread the oils from his hand onto her core, slathering her delicate inner lips, her nub. Her juices and the oil becoming one.

"Which do you offer to me, Mercy," he asked as she writhed against his hand. "Your breasts, sore still from the nettles." He cupped them, caressed them until they were slick and glistening. "Or your eager womanhood..." He stood back, looked down at the stark beauty of her. "...spread so wide and lustful before me..."

He turned from her, retrieved the crop and flogger from their hooks on the wall. "Which will receive the lash?"

He stood before her again, passed the crop to Abigail, and draped the flogger over Mercy's shoulder, the leather tails caressing her like fingers. "Which will be spared?"

Gently, he brushed it over her breasts, her belly. A light kiss of the tails against her, back and forth, up and down. From her shoulders, across her collarbone, to her breasts, and her belly again.

He dragged it lower in a new path down to her thighs, then up again, the swing of his hand more forceful, the slap of the leather greater than its sting. The rhythm soothing. Each twist of his wrist now flicking it faster, harder, raking it over her with more force, the ends leaving slight red trails in their wake.

She gulped in breath after breath, whimpered and trembled, and he flicked the ends to her sex, making her cry out, twitch. Tense. Shiver. All at once. Then silence.

"You will hold your lust, Mercy." He eased closer to her, touched her with no more than his breath. "Should you not satisfy my needs...neither shall your need be satisfied."

He pulled away, leaving her wanting. Watching as she willed need away, and breathed slowly again, fully, her eyes heavy upon his once more.

He turned to Abigail, exchanged the flogger for the crop then aimed for Mercy's oiled core. With a scream certain to rouse the mob beyond the manor walls, her legs trembled, tensed and he struck a second, third time bringing guttural cries of yearning from deep within her chest. Her nub swollen with desperate need unspent.

Her head lagged back, her mouth agape, gasping in breaths, her breasts with their hard little nipples taunting him, as eager for attention they were as Mercy herself.

He stopped the strikes, cupped his hand to one, flicked the nipple, pinched, caressed, slapped the crop to it until even its lovely pink ring swelled as though pleading for more. Her cries becoming one long delirious moan. He turned to the other breast, granting no mercy.

Every pinch of his fingers, every smack of the crop, making her shudder, sigh. He turned to Abigail, beckoned her closer. She held a hand flat to her chest as though to calm her heart, her gaze, fixed on Mercy's breast as he soothed it.

"Do as I do, Abigail," he said softly.

Hesitantly, she reached out, brushed just her fingertips over Mercy's other breast. The touch fleeting yet potent for Mercy as she gasped, seeming shocked by the added sensation.

"Your mouth, Abigail," he said, cupping his hand to the back of her head, forcing her toward Mercy's breast. "Soothe her further...as I had soothed you."

She did not resist but closed her sweet lips over Mercy's nipple in the lightest kiss, the sweetest lick, his own mouth growing dry at the sight.

Her tongue darted out, flicked the pebbled bit, sending a pulse of wet need through him. He could not subdue it but resisted the urge to grip himself through his breeches, to hold tight. He breathed deeply instead, tamed the need he should not feel yet could not deny. And then he reached for Abigail. Pulled her from Mercy.

She looked at him, those beautiful innocent eyes now clouded with her own desire.

Mercy. Elizabeth. Their beauty exceeded that of all others. Yet it was Abigail who pulled at something inside of him. Abigail, a beauty herself though not fully realized. Like the bud of a flower. Timid in the sun and sipping the rain, while the full bloom beside it spread itself to the light, and swallowed the rain whole, knowing what it needed and taking it...

He drew her closer to him, ached to take her now, her mouth, her breath, her body.

Her small hands clutched at his clothes, her need as sure as his. Yet the time was not right to quench such desires. Nay, this time, these moments, were for Mercy. Not his own greedy lust.

He tightened one hand on the crop and covered Abigail's with the other, forcing himself to pry her hands from him.

He turned to Mercy. Her heavy gaze fixed on them, fatigue clear, desire clearer as she looked from him to Abigail.

He cupped Mercy's core, probed her, felt her wetness drip into his hand, imagined how wet Abigail would be at the moment, her desire tame yet potent...

Mercy shivered. Her muscles contracted around his fingers as they pushed her near the edge. She suffered. He saw it clear in her eyes, her stance. Her crimped brow and puckered lips showing her desire to control this longing.

Pleased by her efforts, he dropped the crop to the floor, wrapped an arm around her, and held her close, his cock, full and eager now, pressed to her hip. "You will look at me." His voice, thick with arousal, rasped from him.

She did as told and he probed her more deeply, his fingers exploring every slick bit of her, probing, withdrawing then probing again. And then he caressed her sweet spread core, her nub so swollen now he believed it might truly pain her.

"You will hold your pleasure," he said as he fought to hold his own. And he pierced her again, two fingers showing no mercy as they thrust in and out of her. His breaths and hers merging until the hot air between them created moisture upon her brow and his.

"Please..." Pain, true and complete, filled her voice. Pain of want. Pain of pleasure denied.

Chapter Seven

Abigail moistened her lips as she watched them. Mercy's eyes, shimmering with tears, looked into his. And his hands, caressing her, holding her, brought her to breathlessness yet again.

"You will hold your lust, Mercy," he said, his voice as strained as Mercy's pained eyes. "Tame your pleasure so it be known 'tis not Satan who rules it."

Mercy whimpered then. Trembled. But did not plead further. Her gaze on his, straining with need.

"Breathe, Mercy. Feel it." He claimed her core, spread wide and glistening, cupping it with his hand.

"Hold it," he said, "…until I grant you release."

Mercy cried out, shook her head in frantic need, as though unable to tame her lust any longer.

Abigail held her breath, certain Mercy would fail this test of Jameson's. Feared Mercy would crumble in his arms, a writhing heap of pleasure spent before its time. With all that was in her, she hoped Jameson would grant Mercy release before that happened. Hoped she would find it by his hand, not suffer the feeling of it just out of reach. That, of all, was Satan's want. A witch tortured by her need, need only the beast, himself, could subdue.

And then he eased back from Mercy, caressed her clamped core with the gentlest touch that made even Abigail gasp, ache. Want.

"Mercy…." His voice was thick with passion and promise. "…now."

Hard, sharp moans gushed from her. Cries of abandon, of passion bursting without restraint. Growing louder until no sound came from her at all, just a desperate gasp and then silence. Her head back, her legs shaking, her chest heaving. Her body, so contorted and wracked by pleasure as Jameson continued the strokes against her, the clamps upon her nether lips snapped free and she screamed, a hoarse cutting sound.

She fell then, knees bent, body limp.

With her own cry, Abigail reached for Mercy.

With ease, Jameson caught her in his arms and lifted her. He carried her to the hearth, her full and luscious body seeming small and fragile in his embrace.

"Twas a moment for you, Mercy," he said softly with no strain in his voice. "You alone."

Abigail followed close behind as he gently laid Mercy before the heat of the fire.

He knelt beside her, deftly removed her collar, her cuffs. "Mercy." He spoke her name as a lover. Soft. Seeking.

She did not stir, and Abigail feared the worst. "She is bewitched?"

"Nay," he said, and brushed Mercy's hair back from her face, caressed her cheek, her arms. "She has endured much this night, 'tis all." He stroked her body with slow gentle caresses of his open hands. "Mercy...you have done well."

Abigail sat beside her, certain Mercy had fainted. Her first touch to Mercy's cheek shocked her. "'Tis as cold as a witch's teat."

"Aye. You will warm her."

She did as told, sitting close enough to cradle Mercy's head in her lap. She stroked her hair, her cheek.

Jameson's hands remained on her body, lightly touching, caressing with tender care and ease.

"Mercy." He said her name in an impassioned whisper, as though it slipped from his tongue in a moment of abandon, though he made no pause. He did not search her face, nor show lust for her body as he drew his hands down her length, from her shoulders, to her breasts, her belly, hips and legs. Then back. "You have pleased me this night."

Her eyes fluttered open as he spoke to her, then closed again as though sleep would not yield.

He left them by the fire and Abigail watched him, his step solid he strode toward the chest beside the chamber door.

Mercy sighed and Abigail gently caressed her. Soothed her. She had known only strength from Mercy. To see her now, so vulnerable, with her wanton ways muted...was to see Mercy's twin, Hannah. Innocent and raw.

Jameson draped Mercy with a blanket of cotton, and she stirred.

"She will recover?"

"Aye," he said softly. "Full and well. Mercy...I will see your eyes."

She drew a long slow breath as with a morning stretch, then opened her eyes slowly and blinked.

Abigail felt her warming, saw her paled cheeks turn pink once again.

Jameson's gaze strayed not from her face. "I had feared your pleasure might be insatiable," he said as he stroked her body through the cotton. "The devil's torment. No sensation. Only need. 'Twas relief to see you sated, and now at ease."

"I..." She seemed unable, unwilling, to speak further, leaving a question unspoken.

He smiled for her. It was true, shining there in his eyes.

Abigail smiled with him, most eager to hear what words he might speak.

"You are unmarked," he said.

Sudden tears filled Abigail's eyes and girlish laughter she could not contain shuddered through her.

Mercy moved as if to rise. Jameson assisted, then eased her to a stool beside the hearth. She held onto him, a hand gripped to his arm, the other holding the blanket to her chest. Her eyes, lazy, half-drawn, on his. She bowed her head as though giving thanks, her gaze meeting Abigail's for the briefest moment before she bowed to her as well.

Relief, most powerful, filled Abigail. Of knowing Mercy's ordeal would now end, of Jameson's hand, though caring and gentle, no longer rousing Mercy, nor being roused by her beauty.

She knelt before Mercy, took Mercy's hands in hers. "Hannah will delight as you join her."

Jameson pressed a hand to Abigail's shoulder and she turned to look up at him, aware she had spoken out of turn, for it was he, alone, who would determine Mercy's release.

"Forgive," she said. "I did not mean--"

He shook his head, silencing her. "Mercy." He showed neither pleasure nor reprimand as he turned from Abigail. "Your ways will not be understood," he said, and his tone no longer held tenderness but resolve and regret. "Your needs will be seen forever as immoral." He held Mercy's gaze a silent moment then slowly shook his head. "You cannot remain here in our Wedick Colony, but must be taken beyond the borders."

Fear clawed at Abigail's throat. "You would banish her?"

"Aye," he said, his solid gaze warning her into silence before he turned back to Mercy. "Your passion is unlike that of the others here. I fear, were I to allow you to remain, you would soon find yourself beneath my hand once again."

Mercy's smile was slow in forming. Soft. Lingering. Seeming to consider the notion. She looked at Abigail then, a slow glance over her face, her body knelt there before Mercy.

Then Mercy turned back to Jameson and drew a long slow breath. "I will have my life," she said, "and so I do not protest this banishment." She breathed a smile. "I welcome it." As quickly, her smile fell. "But I shall not be removed from my sister without quarrel."

Jameson gave her a single nod. "She will be sent as well." He turned to Abigail. "Remain here, with Mercy. See to her comfort, then bring her to me." The caress of his hand against Abigail's face was so light, a mere flutter against her, that shivers coursed through her. "I will see to Giles now," he said.

"And Elizabeth?" she asked, searching his eyes. They darkened, more with regret than anger, and though she wished to plead again on Elizabeth's behalf, her voice would not sound.

"Should Mercy need what you cannot provide," he said. "I shall be but beyond the door." He entered the other chamber and closed the door between them.

Mercy covered Abigail's hand with her own. It was cool, despite the warmth of the fire beside them. "Your heart will do well with our governor."

"You will do well to watch your tongue." Abigail bit her own for such a bitter retort, her fear for Elizabeth foremost on her mind, though no excuse. She turned to Mercy, who laughed softly and caressed a hand to Abigail's cheek, the gesture not unlike Jameson's.

"Do not fret so, Abigail," she said. "I tease you not, for you have won his heart." She leaned closer, released the blanket covering her breasts, and cupped Abigail's face in her cool hands, the touch gentle. Her voice a whisper. "You have bewitched him."

With a slow shake of her head, Abigail responded the same. "I am not a witch."

"Nay." Mercy held Abigail's gaze as she had not done before. Not studying, not challenging, but...seeing. She stroked Abigail's face, her neck. Light caresses that tingled, fluttered deep within Abigail's belly. Mercy's expression almost reverent, as though Abigail had somehow impressed her. "You are not a witch."

Abigail shook her head slowly, her gaze locked on Mercy's. Then Mercy leaned closer, and Abigail did not recoil, taken was she by the tenderness in Mercy's eyes.

Mercy leaned closer still, closer until her lips met Abigail's, a slight brush at first then a light moist pressure. The feel of them, the softness, the warmth, unexpected. Sweet and stirring.

Abigail closed her eyes and returned the gentle kiss, leaning in for more even as Mercy withdrew.

"You are a woman," Mercy said, her heavy gaze dripping toward Abigail's mouth. "As such, you are more powerful than any witch could ever be." She smiled in that natural, knowing way of hers, then turned to warm her hands by the fire. "'Tis why we are here," she said. "'Tis what frightens them so."

☙❧

Jameson took in the sight before him, of Giles and Elizabeth, gazing at each other. Their voices, hushed. Low murmurs, only. 'Twas the tone of lovers, each speaking for no one but the other. The sound, the sight, intimate. As though they — bound, naked, and accused — had no cares beyond these walls.

He closed the chamber door behind him and they turned. All sense of peace dissolved as though he, Jameson himself, brought darkness to them.

Perhaps he did, for their fate rested upon his decree. Though he loathed to declare Elizabeth marked, he had no proof to the opposite. Neither proof nor hint beyond Giles' word.

Elizabeth studied him now. The fire in those green eyes of hers darker, subdued. Either resigned was she, or unaware of her fate, while the unease in Giles' eyes told how well he knew.

"Dawn nears," Jameson said, painfully aware how little time remained. "And with it, judgment."

He went to Giles. An innocent wronged. Jameson would take these precious few moments to help his friend as he had vowed. To rouse him. To show him he was the man he thought he was not, yet Jameson knew him to be. He had but this time, for no other would present Giles so bare, so vulnerable...nor would it present the proximity of the woman who roused his needs. This woman, condemned.

Jameson stood eye-to-eye before his friend and pressed a hand flat to Giles' chest. He felt the heat of him. The hard steady pounding within, the scratch of light coarse hairs against his palm.

"I shall keep my vow to you now, my friend," he said to Giles, "and prove you are as able as any man, no matter the tortures of the past."

"Elizabeth…"

Jameson resisted the urge to look at her again. "She has determined her own fate," he said, wishing it could be another way.

The pounding grew fierce beneath his hand.

A muscle worked in Giles' clenched jaw. His voice came thick and low. "I would take her from this place…"

"You would be hunted," Jameson said. "And you would be found." With care and deliberate ease, he stroked his hand up over Giles' chest to this throat. He gripped it lightly, lifted Giles' chin, and held his gaze. "And others, accused, would stand with no watchman to protect them…nor with a governor, such as I, for it would be said I aided in your escape." He shook his head slowly and took a step closer, until no space existed between them. "That I cannot allow." Nor would he permit.

Giles made to speak and Jameson gripped tighter, accepting no argument, no resistance, remaining so until satisfied none would come. Then he unlocked the shackle at Giles' wrist.

"You do not bear the devil's mark," he said and led Giles toward the large table. He took the oil from the pouch on his hip and set it on the wooden surface. "Yet you bear others." He stroked his hand over the scars at

Giles' back. "These are marks I cannot take from your flesh," he said, "but wish to purge from your mind."

He stood beside Giles, whose gaze strayed toward Elizabeth. And then Jameson glanced her way himself.

In silence, she and Giles looked at each other. Secret thoughts exchanged.

"She rouses you," Jameson said, then poured several drops of oil into his hand. "Your body…and heart?" His hand slick, he reached between Giles' legs and cupped his soft sac, held it loosely, waiting for Giles to release the sudden breath he drew.

It hissed from him and he drew another, slowly. "As no other before," he said on the release of that breath, his gaze never leaving Elizabeth's.

The strength of Giles, poised and controlled, the power of his arms, his legs — all thick with muscles solid and defined — was a potent sight. Stirring in its might though contrary to the pain Jameson now knew lay within him. Pain that kept his cock from waking even at this moment, as Jameson gripped it in his oiled hand, stroked gently, slowly, completely from its soft base to its wanting tip. Even as a red-haired, green-eyed beauty stood naked just feet away, gazing upon him.

Though perhaps her gaze proved too much to endure.

Jameson turned Giles toward the table and pressed a hand to his back. He felt each tense ripple of muscle as he urged Giles forward over it until he rested with his chest to the wood.

Jameson oiled his hands again, drew a flattened palm down the length of Giles' spine. A firm caress to the curve of his rump and below to his testes hanging there. Soft. Yielding to the gentle pressure of Jameson's fingers upon them.

"'Tis not your body which betrays you, Giles," he said, wishing Giles might think how Elizabeth had roused him. How her nearness stirred that which had slept so deeply within him for so long. "'Tis your mind."

He drew a finger backward, pressing well against Giles' perineum. Stroking firmly, aware the feeling could push Giles' too quickly or not at all, yet eager was he to see some response from his friend.

"Close your eyes, Giles," he said. "Do not think, but feel." He waited for Giles to do as he said, then reached forward with his other hand, lightly gripped Giles' sac and cock, pulsed his hand to them in a gently rhythmic way, slowly stroking and squeezing, holding, aware how little time they had, yet rushing not. His touches deliberate. Careful. Controlled.

He felt the slight weight of Giles' testes against his palm, rolled them in his hand, curled his fingers around them, like a ring, and gently tugged. Welcoming each tremor from Giles and each gruff breath he expelled.

He released him to reach over the table and take a long strip of leather from the shelf above it. Gently, he gripped Giles' cock and sac again and wound the leather strip around them, at the top of his testes and base of his cock. He tied it firmly yet not overmuch, his wish to trap Giles' pleasure so it would not fail him so easily.

"For pleasure only," he said as Giles startled. "Not meant to harm in any way."

He held Giles's bound sac and palmed his buttocks with his other hand, felt the muscles there tense and flex, and then gently he pressed an oiled finger to Giles' anus, wishing to reach inside of him as before. To stroke that tender spot within and to see Giles succumb to the pleasure of it.

He smoothed his finger over the fine hairs there, circled it over that tight hole not untouched, spreading the oils well. Softening the muscles. And then he pushed on, slight pressure. Then more until he pierced Giles with the tip of his longest finger. He held still a moment so Giles' body might accept this intrusion. And then eased further inside, pushing past the tight hot resistance there, savoring the sound of Giles' low moan. Slowing when Giles tensed further, his muscles contracting, gripping Jameson. Stopping further access to this dark and hidden heat.

"Widen your stance," he said and urged Giles' feet farther apart with his own.

Giles' complied, his legs spread wide, his hands clasped so tight on the table before him his fingers went white. His want clearly to respond as a man should respond, to accept these touches though his body chose not to comply.

Yet with body and thoughts at war...

Jameson glanced back at Elizabeth, certain Giles' thoughts strayed to her, as did his own.

Her gaze lingered on his hands against Giles, yet no sense of it appeared in her eyes, as though she looked but did not see. Her thoughts, no doubt, lost to her fate, as were his and Giles'.

He turned back to his friend. Saw the pain in his eyes as he, too, looked toward Elizabeth.

Jameson leaned closer, blocking Giles' view of her, and pushed on. Probed him deeper. Slowly to the second knuckle, slipping carefully inside of this most secret spot within his friend. Wishing to bring his thoughts back toward pleasure.

He held steady there, not rushing, entering further only when Giles' muscles eased. Then, gently, Jameson twisted his wrist, turning his finger within his friend, until he found the spot he sought. That small swollen knot of hidden desire.

He pressed it with the tip of his finger. Stroked as he would like it stroked for himself. A touch, firm. Steady. Enough to send a rush of want straight to the head of his cock, to make it throb as it sprang to life…

Giles tensed. Ground out a low moan. His legs unsteady. His cock twitching only. Seeking that which still lay well out of reach. He shook his head. Rocked it back and forth. Then glanced at Jameson, frustrated need clear in his pained eyes.

Jameson stroked more firmly, pressed down on that sweet spot with purpose.

Giles bucked, heaved a growl through clenched teeth, the sensations clearly too much, yet not enough.

"Calm," Jameson said softly to him, aware he caused more grief than delight.

Even Elizabeth cried out, pleading for Jameson to cease all he did to Giles.

He eased the pressure within his friend, wishing him only pleasure, though aware in this moment pleasure would not be found.

"I have failed you," he said and the weight of that truth hurt his heart. He inched his finger from the tight recess until he touched his friend no more. The burden of this failure slowed his step as he went to the hearth.

With water, hot from the kettle, he washed his hands, then dried them by the heat of the fire. "I sought to help, Giles," he said, his gaze on the flames, low now, crackling like winter twigs under foot. "Yet this time is not right to awaken you."

Pain, deep and unreachable, laced Giles' harsh breaths, and Jameson turned from the withering flames to face him.

He stood before the table, head low, palms flattened to the wood. "I care not for my own pleasure," he said, "but for Elizabeth's life."

"Please!" Elizabeth cried. "Think not for me, Giles...'tis your pleasure..." Unshed tears thickened her voice. "I would please you again...I would submit...now... should I be permitted..."

Her glance toward Jameson was quick yet potent, and he felt the true passion of her words.

"It is my pleasure..." She flattened a hand to her chest as though it hurt to speak, to breathe, "...my pleasure which pleases you, Giles...and so...I submit..." Those vibrant green eyes turned to Jameson, tears of compassion spilling from them. "'Tis too late for myself," she said, her trembling voice now an impassioned whisper, "yet, I beg you...grant me this request."

He felt an urge to laugh in relief at that moment, for the heart of a witch, truly bound to darkness, would not know such grace or benevolence.

He drew a slow breath to steady himself. To determine whether he now witnessed purity or deceit.

"You submit to me here...now..." He went to her, one slow step at a time, eager to awaken her, for to please her would be to please Giles. Of this, he was certain. "You submit to all I do...to all I say..." He stood before her then, looked down at her, searching her gaze. "...with no thought to resist?"

She shook her head. "Aye."

"For our Giles," he said, aware how well her heart challenged her mind.

She made to look around him, but he did not move, and she closed her eyes. "For Giles," she said in a whisper.

And for Giles, he would accept what she offered, dark or pure. He smoothed a finger over a smudge at her rib, making her flinch. "This is but one scratch of many upon your flesh," he said. "How many hands have touched you this night?"

She seemed to shudder. "Many."

"Lecherous and cruel, they were."

"Aye."

They left not only the mark upon her thigh, the mark they called the devil's, but shadows of their clawing touches as well. He could have spared her that fate had she submitted to him then... as she submitted to Giles. Lest that, too, be a means to deceive.

He clasped her chin in his hand, forced her to look at him. "Giles touched you as they did."

"Nay. Not as the others," she said, fire in her eyes. "Gentle was his touch."

"You permitted it."

She did not look away, did not blink. "Aye."

"You sought it."

"Aye."

He let go of her face, dropped his hand to her waist, then strode behind her, dragging his fingertips across her belly, over her side. He would rouse her for Giles now, yes. Yet he would test her word as well, to assure himself that her heart lay as bare as she.

He gripped her from behind, his hands at her hips, and leaned closer to her. "You sought to bewitch him."

"Nay!" He held her still when she would have spun to face him. "'Twas to prove my innocence."

"Yet you are here," he said. "In my chamber. Deemed guilty by all those beyond the manor walls." He ignored her protest. Glanced up at Giles and noted the tension in his stance, the question in his eyes. He wished for Giles to know that he would as much permit her to rouse him, as he would examine her for the mark. His heart angry with her for causing such distress for so many, though not willing to condemn her should she be innocent.

He drew her backward, toward the wall behind them.

She did not resist, yet did not yield. Her step awkward, stumbling, her back to his chest, the shackle at her ankle clanking angrily.

He still held her. "By what means would you have proved innocence, Elizabeth, had Giles not defended you so?" he asked. "Would you lie? Feign pleasure to fool our Giles and awaken him as no other could? Even submit to me in these last moments?"

"I do this not for myself —" She cried then, ragged breaths and tears he did not expect. "Giles, 'tis my vow. I do this for you."

He admired his friend, standing there, watching in silence, breaths of concern and compassion filling his chest, making it swell and deflate, slow, steady, as though he struggled to control it. As though he understood what Jameson did here, yet hated him for it in that moment, hated, as well, Jameson's hands on Elizabeth, yet even himself seeing no other way.

"He is a man of honor, our Giles," Jameson said. "And he would defend yours."

"'Tis why he is here." She made no effort to wipe her tears. "'Tis for me."

He dipped his head toward hers and spoke softly into her ear. "And now this be for him."

Her slow full breath failed to calm her trembling. "Aye." Her small hands reached back and clutched at his legs behind her, her fingertips digging into his thighs, high near his hips. Her grip firm. Panicked.

Resigned.

"Calm, Elizabeth," he said softly, wishing now to soothe her so she might soothe Giles. He wrapped an arm loosely around her waist, pleased more by her submission at this moment than of all those before her. "On my word, you have naught to fear within these walls."

"Giles spoke well of your honor."

He breathed the smallest laugh, aware Elizabeth's faith lay not in his word, but in Giles'.

He leaned back against the wall and set his legs between hers, then widened his stance, forcing her legs farther apart. Allowing Giles this most intimate view of her.

"'Tis only pleasure you will feel now, Elizabeth." He flattened his palm low on her belly, smoothed firmly over the front of her silken hip and on to that sensitive crease where her thigh met her unshaven mound. He curled his fingers over the fullness of her upper thigh, his knuckles grazing her nether lips as he gripped her lightly. "Pleasure which bears no shame," he said, "nor challenge to honor."

She trembled in his embrace but did not try to stay his hand.

"Open your eyes," he said, his own shifting from her to Giles, who watched her closely. "See how he looks at you." Gently, he grasped her jaw with his free hand so she might look Giles' way. "You please him, Elizabeth. Your beauty and abandon."

He strummed the fingertips of his other hand through the tight red curls veiling her treasures, bringing Giles' attention there. Then he dipped into her heat, a light brush of his fingertips between her swollen nether lips. Cold she was, yet moist, despite her unease.

His fingers wetted, he circled them gently over her tiny nub. Held her more firmly as she bucked. Continued with light strokes against her, barely touching, an unrelenting tease against this tender bit of her. Enough to make her tense further. To desperately knead his thighs. Whimper. And then he combed his fingers through her sweet tangled thatch, spoke softly to her. "Tell me, Elizabeth, did he touch you this way?"

She made to speak but no words came from her lips.

He looked at his friend, saw the tight set of his jaw, certain it was as much from want as frustration, for Elizabeth's discomfort was plain despite her brave efforts. "Was it the sight of her, Giles, the feel of her which roused you?" He kept his voice low, calm. "The sound of her sighs?" Unwilling was he to stir this air so tense. "Tell me."

Giles stood at his full height, his full strength. His gaze, probing. Questioning. Softening with each caress of it upon Elizabeth.

"I was cold," she said when Giles did not respond. "And frightened. Bound alone in the dark forest."

Giles nodded, his step slow as he approached.

"He offered comfort," she said, "when I felt despair."

"You ordered her bound to the great oak," Giles said, taking his gaze from her for only the briefest glance at Jameson. "Yet her eyes pleaded... and as two watchers cowered in the brush beyond — Mary and Samuel — both certain evil would show itself in Elizabeth's form, I sought to expose her innocence."

"How Giles? Show me."

"You are as the oak to which I secured her," Giles said, "spread wide, full against the bark, as I touched her, as I felt her heat. Her passion." He gripped her arms, his fingers biting into her flesh though she did not cry out. "Turn to him," Giles said, and she complied without hesitation. Her lovely body, soft full breasts, gently rounded hips, there willingly before Jameson. Stirring, though it should not be, for these moments were for her, for Giles, alone.

Jameson lifted his gaze to her eyes, averted they were, looking beyond him to the wall. And then Giles grasped her wrists, and raised her arms, flattening her hands to that wall on either side of Jameson, forcing her body against his. The feel of it, the softness, further threatening his control.

He gripped her hips, eased her from him until he could breathe again.

Giles' gaze lingered on his as though knowing Elizabeth's effect on him, sharing it purposely. And Jameson relented, willing to see the proof Giles would show him, even with time so fleeting.

"Touch her as you did, Giles," he said. "Touch her…now…rouse her well in these moments before dawn."

A need for assurance lingered in Giles' gaze and Jameson gave him a single nod. "Judgment has yet to be made," he said, certain this hope to prove her unmarked would free Giles of further concern, further barriers to his own pleasure.

"Elizabeth…" Giles' breathed her name, a sound both thick and tender.

His name floated on her sigh in response.

Giles wasted no time. He wrapped his arm around her waist and drew her hips to his. The shift locked Jameson's hand between Giles' solid thigh and Elizabeth's succulent flesh.

She dipped her head forward, all but resting it on Jameson's shoulder, her hair falling about her face.

"Tell me, Giles," he said, his own voice thick. "Be she cold and dry…as the witch…or does she drip for you?"

Giles closed his eyes, leaned into her softness, threatening to crush her to Jameson.

"Elizabeth…I…" There was pain in Giles' voice. Apology.

"Please Giles…tell him true…" She ground out the words, whether from shame or need mattered none, for she struggled, eager to please, not to resist.

Giles shifted, his gaze full on Elizabeth from behind, his hand reaching down where Jameson could not see.

Her breaths came hard, and she touched her forehead to Jameson's shoulder.

He held her more firmly, certain Giles' fingers lay buried inside of her.

"She is as a leaf drenched in morning dew," Giles said. "Chilled as though eager for warmth."

"Warm her, Giles. As you did before."

Giles' free hand smoothed over her waist to her hip, brushing over Jameson's hand gripped there. And then he smoothed upward again, the strength of Giles well controlled. He cupped Elizabeth's breast. Held her as though she were most fragile, thrummed his fingertips over her nipple until it stood firm and proud as she. The paleness of her flesh blushed beneath his touch, gentle though unyielding as he squeezed, caressed. Her fullness molding itself to his hand, the softness of her flesh a clear pleasure for Giles.

She sighed, writhed against Giles, whose eyes closed softly. And Jameson held her more firmly. His knuckles brushing Giles' thigh, the coarse hairs scratching the back of his hand, latched still, onto Elizabeth's hip, his fingers pressed to her hot plush rump. He held her back further from him, would not permit her to brush against him, though he ached for the contact, the release, as his own pleasure surged. The passion of these two, the heat of their breaths, their bodies. Their need and want...

"Yes, Giles," he said, the agony of his friend's pleasure clear on Giles' face. His lips thin, brows gathered. "See how she writhes for you."

Giles' brow knotted further, and he squeezed her breast in his fist. Caressed. Brushed his hand forward and pinched, pulled her nipple. Making her cry out in clear desire. Stirring her, as well, with his other hand unseen, until she clutched at Jameson's arms, her head still pressed to his shoulder, sharp coos cutting though her tight breaths.

Jameson shifted, took her head in his hands, smoothed her hair from her face. "I will see your eyes, Elizabeth," he said, his words a breathless whisper. His own desire pulsing beneath his breeches.

Giles gripped her hair, pulled her head back, his voice gruff as he spoke against her ear. "Do not hide," he said, "Permit him to see you as I do, Elizabeth...you must..."

Her eyes opened, though barely. Lust, rich and dark, deepening their color to the shade of evergreens. Pride, even richer, shining in them as they met his, her gaze compliant yet sure.

He brushed his hands back further, dislodging Giles' fist from her hair, watching his friend, relishing the desire upon his face.

He shifted then, disentangling himself, legs and arms, from them. The ache in his breeches building, paining him now, while the tightness in his chest pleased him, for it swelled in relief. Relief for Elizabeth, her passions true, heated in ways incompatible with the witch. And for Giles…

Jameson stood beside his friend, a hand firm upon Giles' back, pleased to see Giles' cock awakened and propped contentedly against Elizabeth's rump.

Jameson's gaze dripped over her, leaning now fully against the wall, her wild mass of curls cascading over her back, the elegant dip of her waist into which Giles' hand stroked, the swell of her hips, her rump, rounded and sitting high on her thighs. And Giles' hand slipping downward again, then further between her spread legs.

Jameson knelt beside them, removed the shackle at her ankle and pulled the chains free from between their feet. Coiled it, brought it to the far wall. Allowing them a few moments alone with each other's heat, flesh against flesh.

He turned back as she cried out, a sound of surprise, her hands grasping now at the wall. Giles did not stop in his caresses, some forceful, some so gentle they seemed impossible from a man his size and strength, his voice low, his words murmured against her cheek as he leaned into her.

Jameson went back to them, warmed by their heat as it pulsed through the air around them. He stood behind his friend, smoothed a hand over Giles' hip then forward over the hollow where his thigh met his groin.

Giles did not flinch but leaned back, into Jameson and Jameson felt the lightness of Giles' heart in that moment, sure as he felt his own.

With a gentle touch, he palmed Giles' cock, felt the fullness of it, the firmness. Then he closed his fist over it, milking him gently, steadily, with more force as Giles pumped his hips in the same rhythm. With his free hand, Jameson felt the ring of leather around Giles' sack, his cock, assuring himself it held firmly yet did not strangle. Then Jameson eased back from his friend, and leaned into Elizabeth, relieved not one in his charge would be condemned this night.

"These moments are for you, Elizabeth," he said in a whisper. "For you have pleased Giles well." Her selflessness, her passion…proof of a heart untouched by darkness, of a body unmarked by the beast. He glanced at Giles, gave him a single nod, watched as Giles' lustful eyes turned relieved, grateful, his brow and posture softened.

Elizabeth shivered and Giles gripped her waist, traveled his flattened hands over her back, up over her shoulders, her arms, raised to the wall. Clasping her hands and blanketing her body with his.

"Elizabeth." Jameson touched a hand to the back of her head, waited for her to rouse fully, to turn her heavy gaze to his. "You are unmarked."

Chapter Eight

Jameson watched Elizabeth closely, assuring himself she heard, she understood, and was not still lost within in the haze of lust.

Tears surfaced and shimmered in her eyes, understanding alighting there. "I am to be freed?" Wonder all but muted her voice.

"Aye," he said with a nod and small smile. "You are unmarked."

She closed her eyes and the flush of desire faded from her cheeks.

For a moment, he feared she might be overcome. "Hold her well, Giles," he said, and Giles gripped her hands more firmly.

"Giles..." She cried softly, sniffling raggedly as though to control the strength of her emotion.

Giles turned her into his embrace and she wrapped her arms around his neck, held him full against her, cried into his shoulder. And he held her. Relief, profound yet tame, filled his eyes before he closed them.

Jameson understood, felt his own sense of calm not for Elizabeth alone, but for Giles as well. He remained within the circle of their heat. Wishing to grant them time alone, yet wishing more to have this night end, to declare all unmarked and see madness fade from the village...at least until the next full moon, until the next group of accused witches were bared before him. Until the next cycle of fear wound its way through the village.

Yet for now...

"These moments are for you, Elizabeth," he said in a whisper. "What do you seek?"

He would see her passions sated, Giles' as well. After the terror she endured this night, he would grant her full pleasure within these walls, as so many innocents before her pleaded for him to do. Yet, tonight, for Elizabeth, those pleasures would not come by his hand. Nay. Elizabeth's passions were not his to soothe.

"Would you have me bring you before all now and declare your innocence?" He gently drew them apart, then turned Elizabeth to face him, his hands gripped to her upper arms, needing her thoughts to be on his words alone. "Or would you remain here a few moments longer?"

He looked pointedly at his friend then, the torture of need clear on his face, the newness, perhaps. The purpling of his straining cock, the blood of desire surging to it, trapped there by the leather ring at its base, assuring his arousal remained...until he chose to subdue it.

Jameson looked at Elizabeth again, waited for her gaze to shift from Giles back to him. Her eyes still moist, her face tear-stained, softened, blushing as though she knew the question he would ask next. "Would you leave now, or remain…and permit Giles to see to your pleasure…and you to his?"

She looked at Giles again, and he only at she.

The creak of the heavy chamber door drew Jameson's gaze to it.

Abigail. Her step faltered as she looked from him to the others. Concern clear in her eyes.

"Mercy?" he asked her.

Abigail nodded, questions quirking her delicate brow. "She is steady and eager to leave."

He sought to calm her fears about Elizabeth yet Mercy came to the door, standing behind her. He stood back from Elizabeth and Giles, their attentions on each other, not on Abigail or Mercy. Elizabeth's tears in plain view, Giles' scarred back to them.

"Giles?" Mercy brushed past Abigail, strode forward with smooth delicate steps, easily displaying the beauty of her nakedness before all. "You are here accused…?"

"Mercy." Jameson snatched her arm before she reached Giles.

Giles turned in that moment, and Mercy's gaze traveled over him, falling hard from his eyes to his rigid cock. With a gasp and a smile of surprise and pure joy, she took a step toward him, but Jameson held her firm.

"You are roused," she said, with a breath lustful and satisfied. "Our governor has a most knowing hand…" Her dark seductive eyes turned from Giles to Jameson, wonder filling them.

Any doubt that coiled within him about Mercy's banishment, calmed, certain was he it would be best for all should she be long gone from this place.

He steered her toward the long table beneath which he had placed her small slippers hours ago. He retrieved them, for they would be all that adorned her when he presented her to the villagers.

His hand still tight on her arm, he took her to the door leading to the hall, then turned back, his question still unanswered. "Elizabeth?"

She stood behind Giles, his breadth shielding her body from view. Her eyes and nose above his shoulder. "I wish to remain a few moments longer."

"A few only," he said. "For dawn approaches." He looked at Abigail.

She lingered at the door between chambers, her hand pressed flat to her chest, her gaze touching on each of them. And then she went to Jameson, her steps stiff, her expression tight, her gaze searching his, silently pleading for answers.

He would sweep her into his arms in that moment if he could, swing her high into the air, hold her close. His relief great, his burdens lifted for now, as none would be condemned by his decree this night. "She is unmarked," he said.

Abigail laughed, a surprised and contagious sound of sheer tearful joy. She took a step toward Elizabeth then stopped, remaining beside Jameson. "I am so pleased, Elizabeth." Abigail trembled, wiped at tears, seeming to shed a weight of emotion too great to bear any longer.

Jameson touched a hand to her arm, held her happy gaze with his for a brief moment. "We must go. Mercy should linger here no longer." He turned from Abigail, guided Mercy with a hand at her back, looking down at her when she twisted to face him.

"I am most grateful for your hand," she said, "for myself as well for Giles."

Jameson opened the door to the hall, ready to lead her through, to end this night. "I shall be grateful on the morrow."

"'Twas Elizabeth." Giles voice was thick. Low.

They turned to him.

He stood as rigid as before, his bound cock proud and alert, his hands at his sides. His gaze on Mercy. "'Twas she who cured me," he said, with the smallest glance back at Elizabeth then to Mercy once again.

Jameson did not have to look at Mercy to know she smiled, he heard it on her breath.

"It appears the charms of women are both loathed and lauded," she said, a wistful tone in her voice. "Would that we knew when or why." She turned to Jameson, a rueful smile upon her lips.

Had the mood of the townsfolk been calm, he would grant her release, not banishment. Yet, with no witches to disparage at dawn, banishment, at least, would satisfy their lust for blood.

"I would see my dear sister now," she said.

"Abigail will prepare her," he said with a pointed look Abigail's way.

Abigail nodded, gave one last look at Elizabeth and Giles, then gripped Mercy's hand tight. They shared a silent moment, those two. So different were they, in so many ways, yet in that instant they seemed as one in heart.

Abigail left and Jameson turned to Giles. Questions lingered in his eyes as well. Giles' glance toward Mercy making those questions clear. Jameson nodded and a twinge of regret furrowed Giles' brow, as always when a neighbor was to be forced from their village. "I trust all is arranged for the banished?" Jameson asked.

"Not all," Giles said, "for I am here, unable to take them to safety."

"'Tis as well you remain here, Giles," Jameson said, a pleasant thought clear in his mind, "for another driver would serve the village better this night." He turned to Mercy. "You will be taken to the edge of town," he said then knelt before her, the slippers in his hand. "With Hannah." He lifted her delicate foot and she held onto his shoulders for support. He slid the other slipper in place then stood before her. "From there you need only reach North River."

He waited, and she nodded, listened.

"A man... two... wait there tonight as on every full moon. They will find you and escort you well beyond our borders."

"These men..."

"They are Giles' brothers. You need not fear."

"Where will they take us?"

"They will decide," he said, having never asked, for it had proved well for him and for Giles that neither knew where Giles' brothers took the unfortunate few so ripped from their homes as Mercy would now be. "You will be safe but you must not speak of your time within these walls, nor must you ever return to the village."

With a slow shake of her head, she closed her eyes, seemed to struggle for words but spoke none.

"Should you speak of this Mercy," he said and waited for her to look at him again. "To anyone...or should you return...then all others...banished...will truly be so, with no one to see to their safety."

She nodded slowly, glanced back at Giles. "They are brothers to Giles?"

"Aye. They are men of honor."

She then turned those dark eyes to Jameson again. "We shall not speak of this night, nor shall we return. That is my word."

With no cause to doubt her, he led her into the hall, then looked back at Giles and Elizabeth. "Dawn will not wait," he said, then closed the chamber door, leaving them for a precious few moments.

⊗≫⊘

With gratitude, Giles accepted the few moments Jameson granted. They would be but the first of a day free of hangings, of terror or tears.

He turned his gaze from the chamber door to the hearth, the fire there now so low, it was of little warmth or light, yet it somehow soothed, comforted. Perhaps it was the feel of Elizabeth at his back. The strength of her compassion for him, despite the looming shadow of her own fate. The strength, too, of Jameson's honor. Never wavering, even in moments of despair. Wishing only to seek truth, to right wrongs.

Giles looked down at himself, his straining cock, an unfamiliar sight, a feeling unlike any other. A wonder he thought to never know. And now, as it lingered, pulsed with the needs of a lifetime, he wanted only to subdue it. To give, not receive.

He palmed the shaft, squeezed. Welcomed the delicious spasm that rippled through him... wished now to tame it. Thought to remove the leather tied to it.

Elizabeth's breaths bathed his shoulder in damp heat and he closed his eyes. Welcomed the nearness of her, the tingle of her flesh so close to the scars at his back. Rousing them as well. Perhaps overmuch. Though eager was he to see to her pleasure and to be pleasured further by her, he feared the brush of her hands against his scars might shatter even that which the leather held firm. His strength not as realized as hers.

"You are most brave, Elizabeth."

"Nay. Not I."

He turned, reached for her, wishing to hold her, to rouse her once more.

She drew away. Strode toward the hearth.

He followed a few steps, then stopped, unsure of her need. "Do you not seek release?"

"I seek it for you." She turned, withering flames at her back, the fire barely crackling now. She glanced at his arousal. "You are cured?"

In these moments, with her near and deemed innocent, he was cured of all ails. "Your pleasure brought mine yet again." He looked at his cock, standing proud and firm, fondled the leather wrapped tight around its base. "With this restraint, I believe it is made to remain."

"Does it pain you?"

He breathed a laugh, for if this be pain, he would accept it gladly. Blissful pressure it was. Always so fleeting for him, a rare gift granted only at brief and random moments in time. "Does your pleasure, unspent, pain you?" he asked.

"It threatens such."

He wanted her, was enthralled by her. Aroused not merely in body but heart. He stepped closer to her. "'Tis my hope, I do not threaten."

"You do not."

He eased closer still, cupped the back of her head in his hand, her lush curls a cushion against his palm. With his other hand at her waist, he drew her to him.

Her palms were cool upon his chest, warmed as they smoothed downward, to his sides…

He braced for the feel of them against his back, for the memories, which always returned through touch. In blinding flashes. The crack of the lash. The screams. The smell of blood. The choking feel of tears unshed.

They did not come. She did not touch.

He opened his eyes, looked down into hers.

Tenderness lingered there, gazing up at him. "I have frightened you."

"Nay," he said. "'Tis my own mind."

He eased her to arms' length so he might see her. How he ached to touch her while she was bound beyond his reach, and now, as she stood before him, there for him to hold, to taste, to have…he wished to savor the moment. To bring her pleasure about slowly, hear her sighs, watch as a flush grew upon her flesh because of his touch.

That would bring pleasure to him, for his comfort lay not with touch upon himself but of his hands upon another. Of his hands upon her. "If we were to leave here now, then time would be ours so we might have more than these few moments."

Her soft smile drew his eye. She turned out of his arms, strode further from the hearth, and he could but watch as she moved. Every step of her long legs, every sway of her full hips, sent her mane of wild tight curls bobbing about her shoulders, her back.

She reached the long table, swept her palm lightly over it and he imagined the feel of it sweeping over his chest, his thighs, tempting him, touching everywhere but where he ached most. Teasing.

She faced him then, breathed deeply, and even that stirred him.

"I would like these few moments," she said, her hand brushing those curls from her shoulder then settling at her throat. "Here with you."

"I will take only that which you offer." He went to her, watched the hand at her throat travel lower, her fingertips skimming her breast as he had urged earlier, as he vowed to do himself had he been unbound.

He took a step closer. "What do you offer, Elizabeth?"

"I offer all for you to take." She smoothed her hand lower, a slight brush of her fingertips over her belly, the ripple of her touch pebbling her flesh in tiny bumps of pleasure, pleasure that made his bound cock reach for her. "I would have your hands against me like so." With a slowness that pained him, she dipped her hand lower still, to the ruddy thatch he wished to touch and taste. "Your fingers thrust inside of me." She stroked the tight curls there, tangled her fingers within them. "I offer all of me," she said, "whatever you wish me to share."

"Spread yourself for me Elizabeth. Share that part of yourself with me."

She did not move and he raised his gaze to hers. Saw desire within it, was certain his held the same haze of need. Her breaths grew heavy, her breasts heaving, capturing his attention.

He strummed his fingertips over the swell of them, gently brushing his thumbs over her nipples until they stood firm. The hard nubs seeming to swell as he held them, lightly pinched them and used them to pull her to him, not letting go even when she stood so close his cock brushed her belly.

"Do it, Elizabeth," he whispered, pulsing his fingers against her nipples, lightly, firmly, stroking them in time to her breaths. "Spread yourself so I might see more of you."

With a sigh, she reached between them, between her legs, and spread herself, her body swaying, his fingers tightening on her nipples, holding her in place. Watching her eyes, then lowering his to see how well she spread herself for him.

"Wider," he said, standing back so he might see.

She adjusted her stance, her feet further apart, her fingers peeling herself open further, exposing glistening, blush-pink flesh from which he wished to sip. Her graceful inner lips were delicately frilled, like petals on the most succulent flower. Her core, weeping with need.

He touched a hand to her mouth, brushed his fingertips over her lips then lightly dipped between them. Her tongue, hot, stroked over them, wetted them. And he withdrew, fitted his hand to her waiting core.

With desire barely tamed, he slid his two longest fingers into her, steadily, yet so slowly, they seemed twice as long, easing yet deeper into her heat. The slickness on his fingers mingling with the slickness of her need. Her body closing around him, the tightness there, gripping him.

His mouth grew dry as she moaned softly. Her breaths, small puffs of heat.

He withdrew as slowly, taking his time, watching need as it etched her face, furrowed her brows, parted her lips further.

His cock ached now as it seemed to plead for the same pleasures enjoyed by his fingers. And then he pulled them from her completely, held them near her core, felt the heat of her as if to draw them back inside. He brought his hand to her lips again, let her taste herself as he had when he examined her in the forest.

She closed her eyes, took his fingers into her mouth, licked them tenderly, until he could take no more and he withdrew again.

"I wish to taste you myself," he said, his gaze on her mouth, his soaked fingers lightly pinching her nipple. Slick against her, the hard little nub popped from his grasp, and he pinched it again. Each time, she gasped.

He glanced down at her core and her fingers no longer spread her but gripped the table's edge as he pinched her. "Do you offer yourself so, Elizabeth, that I might dine?"

"Aye…" she breathed.

He touched a hand to her neck, tilted her chin up with his thumb. "I bid you spread yourself," he said, leaning in, his lips a breath from hers. "You will remain so, should you truly offer that part of you."

Her breaths, heavy and moist, mingled with his. Steady and hard they were. Her gaze, unblinking on his. And then she shifted, smoothed her palms back to her core and he watched, looking down, waiting an eternity for her to open herself to him once again.

And then she gripped her swollen lips between her fingers and tugged them wide. Giving all of herself to him.

No hesitation, no fear.

He tipped her head to the side and sunk his teeth lightly into her neck, a small bite that barely grazed the skin. Her gruff breath urged him on and he nipped and laved his way from her neck to her shoulder, then down to her breast. Gently nibbling the sweet tender flesh there. Gliding his tongue lower to flick her nipple, the firmness rough against his tongue. Each sweep of it over her made her tremble, this touch, his touch, pleasing her.

He closed his lips over this sweet tender bit of her, suckled in slow rhythmic pulses, drawing it further into his mouth. And then he nibbled there as well, her sighs thrilling to him, urging him to nibble more, to scrape his teeth along the tight nub until it slipped free of his bite. Relishing the way she writhed there before him, unsteady now on her feet.

He slid his hands down over her silken body as he eased to his knees before her. Gripping her hips, he inhaled her lust. Rich and inviting. Then he tasted her with just the tip of his tongue, a slow savoring lick along the outer lips she held, over her fingertips there, brushing well between each, then on to her sweet inner lips. The slightest lick then tiny flicks against that delicate bit of her. Then higher, a mere taste, barely a brush against her swollen nub despite the pleading twitch of her hips.

He did the same to the other side, breathing her in, caressing her with his tongue, tender, light flicks to her sweet flesh. And then he dipped into her into her quim, dripping there, seeking his attention.

Her taste was warm and decadent, like earthy wine upon the lips. Earthy wine of which he would sip again, with the same slowness, drinking her in. Easing his tongue inside of her again, feeling her quiver as she stood.

He eased back so he might gaze upon her, then nestled closer again and swept the flat of his tongue over her, tasting all she offered at once, licking, lightly nipping. Gently probing the tip of his tongue to her nub until sharp unsteady moans came from her.

He pressed a small kiss there upon that straining bit and rose from his knees, raking his hands over her body until he stood before her again. Looking down at her as she looked up at him, her eyes dark, heavy.

Wanting more of her, he touched his full length to her, allowing himself that pleasure. Taking her heat. His chest pressed to her soft breasts, her womanhood, still spread, enveloping his straining cock in a hot wet hug.

He shifted his hips, his cock gliding between her spread lips, its length caressing her nub then retreating, only to caress again.

She sighed and he opened his eyes, took in the beauty of her face, eyes softly closed, lips parted.

He touched his forehead to hers, looked into her eyes when they fluttered open. "Does this please you, Elizabeth?"

"Aye."

"Then do not keep that from me."

"Nay... never."

"What more do you seek? What more might I provide?"

"I would taste you...Giles...as you tasted me."

He slid a hand from her luscious body to his cock, cupped himself, stroked. Tensed at the steel feel of it in his hand, at the frissons of need tightening his scrotum and rising up to the bulging head. He rimmed his fingers over a most sensitive spot beneath it, gripping tight, relieved he had not removed the restraint for the fullness of him remained.

He touched his other hand to her cheek, slid his thumb over her lips, found it impossible to look away as the tip of her tongue came out to meet it. Dabbed at it, circled it.

"You would do this?" he asked.

"Please..."

He plunged his thumb into her mouth, watched, mesmerized, as her lips closed over it, drew it in further, her teeth lightly holding it in place, her tongue circling it, devouring it.

The sensations nearly too much, he pulled his finger from the heat of her mouth. And then he snatched her hair in his fist, felt the rush of her gasp, her breath of surprise, against his cheek.

Though eager for this, for her luscious mouth upon his cock, he feared he might deflate as she closed her lips over him, as he had many times in the past. Her gaze was steady on his, near pleading as much as the head of his cock pleaded for this chance.

He gripped her hair tighter, she winced but did not resist as he pulled more firmly. Downward, and lowered herself to her knees before him, her hands gripped to his hips, her mouth bathing his cock with the moist heat of her sweet breaths.

He grasped his cock at the base, over the leather bound there, and held himself out to her. Watching anxiously as she moistened her parted lips with her tongue then closed them over the tip of him.

He thought he might fall to the floor as he slid slowly into the inferno that was her mouth. Bracing his feet wider, he cupped her head in his hands, held on, urging her closer so she might take more of him. And she did, her lips sliding down further, his cock seeming to swell even more, blood cursing through his body, rocking him. Her tongue swept over his needy head, swirled over it, round and round until it throbbed. And then she swished it along that tender ridge.

Lights, blinding they were, flashed behind his eyes. He breathed deeply, struggled for each bit of air as he looked down at her and she lifted her gaze up to his.

She pulled back then, just a bit and clasped his hands clutched there on her head. He did not resist as she moved them, settling them at his back. He held them there, hand in fist, looking down at her as her gaze remained on his. And then she gripped him again, one hand circling his cock just before her lips, the other clutched to his rump. Her delicate fingers firmly squeezing the flesh there as to ease the tension of his muscles, to soften them, to soothe. And then she took him further into her mouth again, more, her lips, her tongue, gliding down on him as though to swallow him whole.

Searing hot tension tightened his sack, made his legs tremble and surged through his cock. It was a flame so fierce he feared he could tame it no longer. He gripped her hair, pulled her back, then dropped to his knees before her, his mouth seeking hers, tasting hers. His tongue dancing with hers in the most decadent way, yet still, it was not enough. He wanted more. Needed more. Would devour her and still not be sated.

Her hands gripped his shoulders as he lowered her to the floor, covered her lush body with his. Whispered her name. Felt her fingertips dig into his arms. And then loosen, caress. A gentle brush of her hands back up to his shoulders, then to the back of his neck.

He opened his eyes, gazed down into hers. Saw the hesitation there but did not answer it, waited. Almost eager now, for even if pain came from her hands to his scars, he would take it, welcome it for he sought her touch.

"Aye," he said softly and then her hands smoothed gently, tentatively over the rippled plane of his back and he could not breathe. Yet he did not die. He felt alive.

His heart pounding so hard he believed it might burst. And still he yearned for more.

Her legs, hot now and restless, wrapped around his, drawing him closer, closer, until the throbbing head of his cock found her heat and dipped inside.

Her quim, tight and wet, stretched around him, a slow yawn of acceptance. Her body slick and eager. Himself shifting slowly, inch by sweet agonizing inch, sinking into her more, and more still, until he could go no further. And he stayed there, their bodies pressed together, thigh to thigh, hip to hip, nether curls as tangled as they. His gaze solid on hers. Not speaking. Inhaling her breaths as she inhaled his, her hands tender against him. Her body hot and pulsing, taking all he gave. Holding him firmly within.

"Elizabeth. I would stay with you, like this, until the morrow. Never withering. For your heat draws me to you as to no other."

"I would draw you further," her voice was a whisper. Her gentle caresses against his scars tingling like luscious pinpricks through to the head of his cock, nestled so deeply within her. Her hips lifted to his, a slight shift, and then she pulled away, just a breath. "I would show you, Giles," she said, "how it feels to know love. To know the touch of another in ways meant to please…"

He knew well of this dance. Had touched many with his hands, his mouth. Every lick, every plunge of his fingers into their welcoming heat brought blissful agony to them, though not so for himself. Yet now…here…

He eased back slowly, wishing not to break this joining. The tensing of her body around him, like a lover's hand wetted by desire, squeezing, allowed him to withdraw yet urged him to plunder her again. And he did. Then eased back again.

As slowly as he withdrew he joined with her once more, pressing his hips to hers, holding them there, pressing further, letting each new sensation fill him. His limbs taut, his sac tight and full. His cock, engorged. Responsive to the slightest shift within her, the same as the flesh on his back, tingling, scurrying heat spreading through him until he felt he might burst from the pressure, the pleasure. And then he withdrew again and plunged back inside of her. Again. Again.

"Elizabeth." Her fingers brushed his back, the prickling sensation stirring his aching cock until it twitched inside of her.

She gasped, eyes closed. "Yes," she whispered. "Please...'tis all of me I give."

He reached between them, reciting a silent prayer that arousal was his and not bound to the leather constraint. He ripped it from himself, dropped it to the floor. Trembled with need as desire pulsed steady and strong.

"You have but to take what you please...Giles...as you please...."

Her gentle supplication, her hot dripping core around him, thrilled him as never before. Buried deep, he sought to sink deeper still and he surged his hips forward, impaling her, grinding his hips to hers, holding her as lust-filled cries cut from deep in her chest. Her head back, her neck, her breasts exposed to his eyes, his mouth, his tongue. His teeth.

He nibbled. Bit. Laved. "Elizabeth." Withdrew from her a mere fraction and plunged within once again. Holding her tighter, wanting to sink into her fully, not just with his tongue or his cock, but with his soul.

And then it grew, this need. This burning desire. A pain as brilliant and blissful as anything he had known, a light behind his eyes, a warmth filling his veins as though his blood absorbed the heat of her core and pulsed it through to his limbs, his belly, his heart, tightening his chest until he gulped in air.

"Giles..." She gripped him from within, her muscles tense and throbbing, milking his cock, pulling him in further. Urging pleasure from him as hers throbbed within her, around him.

With all his might, he held on, not wanting this moment to end, this beautiful moment of agony that made her writhe in tormented pleasure. Her body shuddering there in his arms, her fingers digging into his marred flesh. Holding him, pleasured by him, gasping, sighing there beneath him. Trembling. Gripping his cock yet tighter, pulsing around him pulling him in deeper.

And then all tension eased from her and she released a long low shuddering moan. And he could hold on no more.

"Elizabeth..."

Her eyes fluttered open and peered up into his.

This moment of bliss, most wonderful, most shocking in its strength, built yet further and threatened to burst from him. Rising up with strength unrelenting. Wrestling all control from him. Tensing his every muscle until it gushed in wave after wave of thick, throbbing release, powerful beyond all he had ever known. He could not breathe. Could not close his eyes. Could not look but at Elizabeth.

Her green eyes gazing at his. Her legs wrapped tightly around him, keeping him locked in place as the last of his seed emptied into her, every drop of it convulsing from him, until he was certain no more existed and did not care.

This one moment, this time with her, was now seared upon his mind obscuring the torment, the torture, the pain of the past, making it seem so very long ago.

"Elizabeth..." Whether he remained there buried inside of her or withdrew, he would still and forever be joined with her.

Her smile was unsteady, sweet and sated and somewhat awed. "The pain of this night...the fear, dear Giles..." Tears spilled from her eyes and he caught them in his hands, brushed them away. "They are forgotten now as I lay here with you."

He leaned closer to her, wanting more of her. Greedy he was now, wanting to savor her mouth as well. Her tears he would dry, her lust he would fulfill, his own he would satisfy with one taste of her lips.

They touched. Her lips to his. The softness of them conforming to his, moving on his. With his. And then she opened to him and he dipped his tongue inside, sweeping it over hers, tasting her and knowing then he would crave this taste for all his days.

Moonset

Jameson stood before the manor doors with Mercy beside him. The outside air, though still cold, had calmed. The villagers no longer stood mobbed together as one, but had split into groups. Some huddled close to others, their voices low, arms wrapped around themselves as to ward off the lingering chill. Some rested against the high fence surrounding the manor while others lazed upon the ground, drowsing as though lives were not changed this night.

The massive wooden X's to which the accused had been spread and bound, though barren now, stood proud, ready to serve yet again. Light and shadows from the villagers' torches writhed in wanton waves over them. The structures' own shadows loomed, undulated upon the lawn and gathered lot. Clear. Ominous. Yet oddly unnoticed.

Movement caught Jameson's eye.

Samuel Stoughton had turned toward the manor, his gaze falling over Mercy. Much like a vulture circling, he came forward. Silent. As to dine upon a carcass before the others discovered its existence.

And then a cry came from someone in the crowd for all to rouse, for the devil's whore now stood before them.

Mercy stood proud. Unfazed by their taunts.

Jameson's pity went to her, though they both knew her own behaviors be the cause.

He moved forward with her, his hand at her bare back. He stopped at the edge of the top step, looking out at the crowd as they fussed and fought for the best place to stand.

A glance at the sky told him time was of the essence and he drew a full breath, ready to call out to them. "Who will clothe this innocent woman?" he said.

A low grumble coursed through the crowd, growing louder, disbelief clear in shouts, wide eyes and slack jaws.

"I call for clothing, warm," he said to clarify, his voice rising over that of the mob, "for a trek far from this place." They quieted and he waited until only the rustle of woolen cloaks and the crackle of flaming torches stirred the silence. "A trek well beyond the borders of our village..." he continued, "for Mercy Paine, with lust insatiable, is hereby banished from Wedick Colony."

A roar of celebratory shouts rose up from those below, and a sound, much like a mocking breath, came from Mercy. And then Abigail came forward, bravely breaking through the mob with Hannah Paine at her side.

A vision was she, Mercy's twin. Pale as a ghostly apparition. A natural smile upon her lips, much like Mercy's. Her eyes, catlike and teasing as well, though void of the challenge ever-present, ever-rising, within Mercy's.

Jameson raised a hand, silencing all. "With our Giles bound within the manor, be there a brave man of honor among you to travel with Mercy...and Hannah...to the edge of town?" He waved his hand toward Hannah, and Abigail strode forward with her, urging her up the manor stairs. "You will not dare linger," he said to the crowd. "Not dare harm these women, yet leave them there alone, as they are, and then return home."

He waited for two breaths. Barely permitted a debate on the matter, then turned to Samuel, locking his gaze on the man most able to rouse the crowd. The man most able to stir them to frenzied heights, even as Jameson sought to calm the fears within them.

"You, Samuel!" he said. "You have shown no fear this night. Eager were you to have a witch linger here among you, bound upon the platform, while I examined our watchman for the devil's mark. Have you the honor...the courage...to see these women away?"

Samuel sputtered, indignation clear. His want, as always, to be the voice above the crowd. This minor task would take that attention from him...and thus grant Giles and Elizabeth a more peaceful release, as was Jameson's wish.

At Samuel's silence, Jameson looked at the villagers gathered before him. He spied the basket maker. The old man's back was rounded, his bony fingers gnarled.

"William Wildes," Jameson called, and the frail old man slowly turned to him, barely balancing upon his walking stick. "Perhaps you have fortitude enough for this journey?"

A wave of laughter, mockery at Samuel, rolled through the crowd. Jameson waited. Certain Samuel's honor would force him to accept rather than see a withered old man volunteer in his place.

"I shall see to it," Samuel said. "On my honor, I will see these whores taken from here, never to return."

"And you will see they remain unharmed." Jameson urged Mercy down the stairs in front of him.

With the crook of a finger, he beckoned Hannah to follow, his gaze locked on Samuel's, leaving no doubt as to the seriousness of his task. "On your honor, Samuel," he said, standing before him, "you will take them to the edge of town, leaving them no closer than the pass before North River."

Women came forward, scuttling between the men, cotton and wool garments in their hands. Jameson did not move, did not watch them go to Mercy, but waited, and then, finally, received Samuel's curt, reluctant nod.

Jameson turned then, to the women who dressed Mercy. They pulled her to and fro. Examined the welts left upon her rump, her breasts. Touched them, murmured both in wonder and disdain, clothed her in petticoats, a shift, bodice and hooded cloak.

He touched a hand to Mercy's arm when they completed their task. "Fear not, Mercy," he said for her ears alone. "You will be safe. That is my word."

Her gaze roamed his face. Fatigued. Amused. "I have no fear," she said, a smile forming. "Not of Samuel." She turned from him to Hannah, clutched her sister's hand and drew her into an embrace.

Jameson turned from them, eager now to see to Giles and Elizabeth. His hope their time together, though soon interrupted, would begin again at another time, in another place, beyond the manor and without the threat of dawn to hurry them.

The creak of wheels silenced the crowd while Jameson climbed the stairs. Abigail joined him as he neared the door, her step hurried as to keep up. From behind them, Samuel barked orders that Mercy and Hannah be loaded into the cart.

Jameson opened the doors to the manor, stood back to allow Abigail inside. "You need not be here now," he said to her, though it was his wish for her to remain.

⊂⊃

Abigail stepped into the manor for yet another time this night. "'Tis my wish to be here," she said.

The dark hall, lit only by candles and the slow fading of night, seemed warmer now. Safe. Yet, despite her new comfort within these walls, concern still filled her. For Mercy and Hannah.

She turned to Jameson as he closed the doors behind them.

He paused when their gazes met, his hand still upon the latch.

A beautiful man he was. Sure of posture, of voice and touch. With this look alone, this glance from him, a flutter stirred within her belly. Yet she had questions. Many. But to voice them would be to question his ability, and that she did not wish to do.

She clasped her hands before her, fingers laced. Sure it best to let her questions rest for the moment. There would be time aplenty to ask them once the sun sat high in the sky and all the accused were free once again.

He dropped his hand from the door, looked at her still, and then the smallest smile tugged at his lips. "I would hear your thoughts."

She lowered her gaze, then lifted it as he approached, even his step stirring her.

The touch of his finger to her chin was gentle, his flesh chilled, his smile gone. "I say it once more only," he said. "I would hear your thoughts." His tone left her no choice but to speak.

"Have you no fear for Mercy and Hannah?" she asked.

He looked at her a moment, his gaze unwavering. "Had I fear, it would be for Samuel." He smiled again. Slowly. A slight though sensuous parting of his lips. A look which took fatigue from his eyes.

She watched them. His eyes. His mouth. Waited for more from him.

He did not speak, but cupped his big hand to her neck, his thumb stroking her cheek. The touch sweet and light. Unburdened. Himself clearly unconcerned, while her heart worried still.

"Beyond," she said. "Once he has left them…how will they fare?"

"With ease, Abigail. I assure you, they will be safe."

She opened her mouth to speak again, to seek answers clear and defined. Answers she knew would not come, for all had been warned not to speak of their time within these walls, nor of the banishment of the unfortunate few.

He dropped his hand from her. His smile fading. Fatigue back in his eyes. "You doubt my word?"

A search for answers should not imply doubt, yet she had doubted him earlier. Had even questioned his fairness toward Elizabeth. "Nay…" she said and looked toward the chamber where Elizabeth and Giles remained. Slowly, as though from sunlight and birdsongs, her heart felt lighter, contentment filling her, for their fates were dark no more. All of the women who had been bound with her, all of the women accused this night, and Giles as well, would face the morrow in peace. Because of Jameson. Never before had she known a man such as he.

She pressed her hand to her chest to steady herself, her pulse quickening with thoughts of his tenderness and wisdom. His knowing hand and strength. Not once did he betray the accused. His touches fair and necessary. His heart set on their pleasure, their freedom. While she...

She thought of Mercy and how in moments she had wished Mercy gone, resented her beauty, Mercy's pleasures so sure and rousing. Her mind should have been on Mercy's freedom alone. As Jameson's mind had clearly been.

"You have honor above all else, Good Sir," she said softly. "I am humbled by it."

His hands were warm now against her, gently grasping her shoulders, turning her to face him. "You weep," he said and brushed tears from her eyes.

They were not tears of sadness but of wonder for this man who lavished attention so well upon all...upon her. She covered his hand with hers, shifted easily to press a kiss to his palm. "I know not why I cry, for I am happy." She closed her eyes, smoothed her cheek against his hand.

"Fatigue claims you," he said softly.

Fatigue. Perhaps. She lifted her gaze to his. "You claim me as well." Warm tears pooled in her eyes again. She blinked them away. "Your hand, though knowing, is patient and kind, for we stood in fear this night and you calmed us. Your wish to find truth no matter the loud voice of fear or anger." Yet, she had been angry with him. Had shouted at him in a moment of her own fear and doubt. Wrong she was for not trusting him. "'Tis a fool who sees not the honor of your heart."

He drew closer to her yet she wanted him closer still.

"Your words, Abigail, they are as a sweet caress." His fingertips grazed her lips as though to capture the words that roused him.

She would caress him again. Perhaps soothe the sting from the words she spoke earlier. Words in challenge to his concern for Elizabeth. She should have known he would not relent until Elizabeth had submitted, until she gave herself to him freely to prove her innocence, for he would not have seen her hang.

Could Abigail go back to her moment of doubt with Jameson, she would swallow her cruel words whole so they might never be spoken. "Long before this night, you stirred something within me. And now, after these hours, I find myself...bewitched...by you, Good Sir."

He closed the space between them. Leaned into her. Brushed her lips with his, whispered against her mouth. "Jameson."

With eyes closed, she breathed his name. "Jameson."

His kiss was gentle, though lingering. A touch upon her lips she did not want to end.

Yet he withdrew. "You have been of great aid to me," he said softly, "a light in this long dark night."

Warmth filled her as he held her, an arm around her waist, a hand flattening to her back, bringing her closer to his heat.

"These tests," he said his gaze, down at her, pained, "are most difficult. Truth, uncertain, hardens the heart. Yet you, Abigail, remained true even as I feared the night would change you."

"I feared the same," she said, needing him to know. "Here, this night, as so many were examined...I confess to you...Jameson...I lusted. Even when your hand…rested upon Mercy…" The sight of it seared through her mind. His hands caressing Mercy's breasts, his fingers gliding into her. Her sighs and writhing… "I did not want to see it…did not want to feel…" She searched his eyes, hoped her words would not anger him.

His gaze was gentle upon hers. "Feel what, Abigail…tell me."

"Jealousy," she said, feeling heat rush to her cheeks. "Desire…'tis shameful, I know, yet I…"

"You have much to learn," he said, tipping his head so close to her she felt his words upon her own lips. "For there is no shame in pleasure, only in lust unrestrained."

She closed her eyes, waited for his kiss. Ached for it. But it did not come this time.

"Passion, Abigail…"

She opened her eyes again, looked into his.

"…is a gift of nature."

"I have learned much about passion this night," she said. His touches had been most passionate, rousing her pleasures in ways she could but imagine. "My own…and that of others."

"There is much more to know," he said.

Mercy knew all. She had pleased him, humored him, aroused him…had aroused Abigail herself, as well. "My desire to know more is great," she said, surprised by the boldness of her own words, her own desires, "should you wish to show me."

He tipped his head to nuzzle her neck, her cheek, his breath hot upon her flesh, his lips exquisitely tender against her, skimming over her face, to her lips, lightly grazing them, withdrawing.

She wished to take more, give more. Touch her mouth to his again, taste him, seek his taste of her.

His hands, so strong so gentle, smoothed over her back to her hips, the slight pressure of them turning her to face the wall. "Lift your skirts, Abigail," he said. "Show me this desire you speak of, for I wish to feel it, to rouse it further in these minutes we have."

With a slight glance back at him she gripped her skirts in her hands, lifted them, hesitating. The wanton display he sought shameful to her, yet she ached to please him, to have him please her. To give him all she possessed. All she was.

She drew her skirts higher, the fabric brushing her flesh, sending tingles through her. Then a slow lick of cool air caressed her calves, her thighs, rousing her.

Her heart felt too large for her chest. Filled it, leaving scant room for air, as she raised her skirts to her waist, fully exposing herself to his eyes.

And then his hands, hot they were, cupped her bare buttocks. "Lean forward, Abigail. Bend only at the waist and press your hands to the wall."

He didn't wait for her to move on her own but pressed one hand to her back, urging her forward, the other wrapped at her waist, holding her back from the wall so she was made to stretch to reach it.

Her arms straight, her hands flat to the cool surface, her rump and her sex bared to his eyes, his hands. He smoothed his palms over the back of her thighs, urging her legs wider. Then he caressed her hips. His hands so hot against her chilled flesh, warming her, lightly squeezing her rump, stroking it.

She sought more of their heat. Their gentleness. Craved his touches. Ached for him to glide a finger into her, to stroke her.

With force, sudden and strong, he smacked her rump.

She cried out, a sound as sharp as the sudden pain. A burning pain he soothed with another gentle caress of his palm. And then another strike, harder, like a whip it felt.

Her cry lodged in her throat. Faded to a sigh as he soothed it again. His hands roaming her body, her entire rump, her hips, her thighs...

"Yes, Abigail...you have much to learn." His fingers danced over her flesh, a sweep from her inner thigh to her core. Touching so gently. Too gently.

She wished for more, moaned softly, beseeching him to stroke where her heat gathered. To soothe the ache he created, as he soothed the ache of his spank upon her rump.

"'Tis more than I can teach you this night," he said, his voice heavy.

She made to speak but could not, her breath trapped in her throat as his fingers teased the eager mouth of her quim. She gasped, sucking air deep into her lungs as his fingers slid into her a mere breath. A rush of need threatened to explode within her, desperate was she to feel his fingers further inside, yet they remained at the edge, torturing her with promises unfulfilled. "Please..."

He shifted behind her and she breathed a word of thanks, beyond ready now for him to fill her, to stretch her as he did before, to spread the heat of himself within her.

And then it came, a slight nudge from the bulging head of his erection against her quim. She braced for it, had accepted it before, with wonder, for the size of him seemed enough to tear her in two.

With gentle though unyielding pressure, he gained entry, just enough to make her tense, anticipate the rest.

Wait for him to move, to join with her more fully. This feeling of need making her dizzy.

He shifted again, his heat blissfully pushing into her, stretching her ever so slowly, making her body convulse around him. Her belly tight. A glorious burning sensation building, tensing her muscles. And his moan, soft, low and gravelly, made her twitch, clench her tender muscles around his shaft, buried now deep inside of her.

He withdrew then, the movement slow, small. Just as slowly, he entered her again. And again he withdrew, filled her. And more, slight movements, quick. In and out of her, until she thought she could take it no longer.

His grip on her hips tightened as though he meant to crush them. The pressure of his fingers, the pain, a delicious sensation. And then he plunged into her, his tight trembling groan one of ecstasy.

She reveled in it, breathed with it, held her own lust so she might feel his, hear his, enjoy his, for it was her body which brought him this pleasure pulsing within her. And then he caressed her hips, soothed the ache of his grip. His fingers gentle upon her once again.

She trembled, her legs, her arms shaking as she held herself this way, her body craving yet more, this desire building beyond anything she had known. Her nub so ripe, so full of need, it ached to be stroked. Even without his touch upon her, she felt the first stirrings of release.

And then he withdrew. Spanked her with strength so full, she screamed, sighed when he spanked her again and again. Her body ready to explode into spasms of bliss. "Be this pleasure or pain, Abigail?" he asked.

In her shame, her passion, she breathed her response, shocked by the truth of it. "'Tis pleasure alone." She trembled there, her arms like liquid. Herself waiting. Her quim aching for his touch as her lungs ached for air.

"Lower your skirts."

She could not move. Could not think, too eager was she for his touch so she might find release.

Another spank. Sharp, hard.

She cried out, the pain fierce. Stinging. His fingernails scratching, like fire against her. His palm then soothing the burn. "Lower your skirts," he said again, his voice low, a rumble from within his chest.

She did as told. Her hands, her body trembling. His seed sticky as it dripped from her. She smoothed her skirts, faced him, brushed her hair from her face. Questions jumbling together in her mind, seeming to thicken her tongue. "I...cannot breathe..."

He nodded, his gaze heated and steady. "'Tis the ache of pleasure denied," he said, standing back from her. "Feel it. Hold it. Think of it, yet do not soothe it, for I wish it to be only my hand that shall. Can you do this, Abigail? Can you deny yourself this pleasure?"

"I...do not know..."

"You will try."

Her legs, her body felt as though it had fallen away, leaving only her core, dripping and pulsing with need. "I...crave, Jameson..."

"As you should, for this be the first of many lessons...should you truly seek to learn more." He clasped her face in his hands, looked at her only, did not soothe, even as she pleaded with her eyes. "Will you tame this lust, Abigail? Hold it so I might taste it later? Or will you permit it to spill from you now...and deny me your pleasure when I hunger for it?"

The shame of this lust heated her face. She was not Mercy, need overtaking thought, breaths... "I do not deny you..."

"Then breathe...slowly...deeply..."

She did as he said, calmed her breaths, willing the luscious heat from her core. Insistent it was, lingering. Another breath, full and deep, loosened its hold though by a mere bit. She breathed again, trembled with a sudden chill.

He smiled down her. A small fleeting sign of his pleasure. Then he stood back, his hands slow to release her. Her body chilled further as he turned toward the door leaving her there shaking. Confused. Needy.

ෆ൬

Jameson pressed his palm flat to the chamber door. Ready to rouse Giles, to warn him his time with Elizabeth had ended. Abigail's ragged sigh drew his attention back to her.

The pained furrow of her brow, her breaths unsteady, were clear signs of her continued struggle against the passion he had stirred in her. Passion so rich he could not look away from it, from her. He felt its power beneath his breeches, even in these moments, so few, since his own release.

He thought to take pity on her, to touch her, for one brush alone, he knew would have her writhing in his arms.

He went back to her. Lazy steps not meant to offer hope but comfort. Though he wished to take her again now, he would prefer to satisfy her beautiful lusts when time was not so fleeting. When he could milk sighs from her with the slowest of hands, the gentlest of touches.

He cupped his palm to her flushed cheek. Waited for her eyes to focus upon his.

"You would do well to leave the manor now," he said, noting the confusion in her eyes. "I shall bring Giles to the yard, and Elizabeth. Pronounce both innocent…"

He thought of the responses from the mob, even with Samuel gone, some would not be convinced neither Giles nor Elizabeth was marked. Perhaps he should have banished Elizabeth with Mercy. For her own safety. To appease the most frightened villagers. Though Giles would then lose her forever.

His brothers would certainly see to her safety, yet share no hint of her destination with him. A most vital secret it was, for if any learned of their treatment of the banished, the banished would be hunted, while Giles, his brothers, and even Jameson himself, would be made to answer for their crimes of conscience.

"The villagers will rouse," he said. "Fight in fear to see Elizabeth punished, for their eyes have convinced them she is marked."

Abigail drew a full breath, released it slowly. Her mind seeming clearer, her attention more upon his words. "They will not argue," she said softly, sweet innocence in her eyes. "They trust your word. They will believe."

"The mark they know lingers still upon her thigh," he said. "I know it to be their mark and must convince them of such. Yet they will fight my word. We know this to be true." With a hand at her elbow, he turned her toward the door. Walked her toward it. "Stand clear of them, Abigail," he said. "I would not see harm come to you."

She turned, touched those small hot hands of hers to his chest. Looked up at him. "You will convince them.

You have truth on your side, Jameson." She smiled softly. "She submitted to you, her pride forsaken. And I saw passion in her eyes…"

"Elizabeth…did not forsake her pride," he said, gripping her upper arms and holding her at a distance. "And that pride remains a wound upon us all."

"I do not understand. You examined her. You proved her unmarked."

"Aye. Because her heart is pure." He released her, had but little time to explain, yet her trust in him, her sweet innocence, demanded truth. "She submitted not to me but to Giles, to spare him when he struggled…" He shook his head at the confusion in her eyes, wanting her to know, to understand. "Such compassion, Abigail, compassion that you have in your heart as well…is incompatible with the witch." He smiled, she did not, and he had no more time to explain. "I will tell them. And they must listen. Go now. Stand well of them should they grow mad yet again."

Her confusion shifted to something different. Perhaps resolve in the face of resistance from the crowd.

Leaving her there, he turned, strode back toward his chamber door.

"Had she not relented…"

He turned at the odd tone of her voice. Tight. Strained.

"Had Elizabeth's heart not been moved by Giles' struggle…would you have condemned her to the gallows?"

He shook his head. "She is unmarked, Abigail. She will not hang."

She took a small step toward him. "You knew her to be unmarked…yet you feared she would hang for pride." She eased yet closer, her movements stiff, almost cautious, and he felt a struggle build within her as within himself, for she questioned him now. Seemed to challenge him, bait him, perhaps, with his own words. And then a flicker of pain clouded her gaze as she looked at him, and her confusion became his.

"Please…Jameson…" she said, her voice a whisper, "I ask again…had she not relented, would you see her hang?"

He thought to remind her of all she witnessed this night, this one night for her, though one of many for him. To remind her of how truth, above all else, mattered most of all. He had shared that with her, confided it to her…yet the darkening of her eyes, the hurt washing over them, the accusations he saw in them now, left him cold, unable to respond.

"You would," she said, turning these quiet moments from clarity to uncertainty for reasons he did not understand.

He took a step toward her then, meaning only to soothe, yet she stepped back, away from him.

"All this talk of honor…" she said, tears filling her eyes. Tears he did not wish to see for it was some event, unrealized, which set them there. "…your honor…and your demand for respect of it…and you would sacrifice her to their lust, to their need for blood?" The hand she pressed to her chest trembled, as though to calm her heart and her hurtful words, yet she spoke them still, passionate they were, and most unfair. "You would grant them that morsel to slake their appetite, when you should want to fight for her, for innocence…innocence I believed you wished to protect."

He would not justify himself to her, for she did not know how deeply he struggled for truth. He would do all to save those he could. He would argue for those he deemed innocent, not spite them for their fears or pride.

"I fight for all, Abigail," he said as calmly as he could, though his own frustrations grew at her words for she now questioned his very purpose; challenged his honor and actions when just moments ago she had praised the same.

He waved a hand ahead of him, toward the door and all those beyond it. "Yet they cannot see light when darkness shrouds their minds—"

"They cannot see light if they are left shrouded in darkness. You cannot enlighten them by not sharing truth but only that which they wish to hear." Her breaths quivered as she drew them and he feared fatigue had claimed her too well, her mind not clear, perhaps his touches, his demand she tame her lust, all rising to torment her, to confuse. "Surely, Jameson, you do not believe that satisfies…that it soothes their cravings?"

Her tears fell, unrestrained, and he thought to go to her, to hold her, to start this talk again so he might explain himself more fully, calm her concerns before they grew. Yet pain and confusion shone so clear in her eyes he felt them to his own bones.

"I think not…for cravings tease…" She sniffed at tears. "Desires tempted with a mere taste do not quench such thirsts but rouse them more…" She smoothed her trembling hands down from her chest to her belly and beyond, to brush her skirts as far as she could reach, "as you roused mine, demanding I tame them. You knew, did you not, such desires would not fade but linger, nay, leap at the chance to taste yet more. So is their hunger. This hunger you would feed…with the blood of an innocent you are meant to defend."

"Abigail...on my honor..." He took a step toward her, would explain fully now, believing it was his silence, his own shameful pride, which now hurt her most of all.

She scurried backward, away from him. "Honor? There is honor not in words formed to appease but in words of truth alone." She opened the door, stood taller, shoulders squared. Drew one full trembling breath after another. "The morrow comes." She lifted her chin. "Good Sir." She smacked at her tears, wiped them dry with angry swipes of her hands. "And with it, judgment." She turned from him then, leaving the manor and pulling the door closed between them.

He stood frozen. Thought to go to her, to drag her back inside so she might hear his words, words from his heart...yet her heart had now blackened to him. And time, too great, had been squandered...for dawn would wait no longer.

His own hand trembled as he raised it to his chamber door. He made a fist, it would not steady. He pounded it to the wood.

"Giles!" he bellowed, and pounded again. "Dawn comes."

The Watchman

Chapter Ten

Dawn

With Giles and Elizabeth beside him at the top of the manor stairs, Jameson urged the crowd to settle. His gaze traveled over all those before him, in search of Abigail, hoping she had taken his warning and stood well away from them. Fearing she may have left the grounds completely, taking with her, his heart.

The restless shifting of the crowd calmed and he touched a hand to Giles' back.

"This man confessed to having lain with an accused," he said, keeping the urgency from his voice so he might present calm even in the face of time so fleeting. "And having done so, had the accused been marked, he would be marked as well." Though they were quiet as he began to speak, they seemed quieter still now. "And so, as I have examined him fully, I ask...who will clothe this innocent man?"

As he wished, cheers rose up from those below. Though they would have seen him hang just hours prior, they would now welcome Giles, their friend, their neighbor, back within their midst. Such was the ill state of their minds.

He led Giles down the stairs yet no one came forward to clothe him.

Petticoats, shifts, and skirts had been provided for the six women accused this moon. Yet, no breeches for a man, as none had been set to be examined. Not until Giles had stepped forward on Elizabeth's behalf.

Jameson's gaze lit upon the midwife and he called to her, sending her into the manor to retrieve Giles' clothes.

"Do not dawdle," he said with a glance toward the sky.

Morning twilight had faded. Dawn had come. Time tested him more this past night than any other. And mere moments remained in which to declare Elizabeth unmarked before the reverend arrived. There was not time enough to first see Giles fully clothed.

Not waiting for the midwife's return, he faced the crowd again. "A cloak for our watchman!" he called, scanning all for such an offering.

There was movement among them. Abigail, precious Abigail, pushed her way forward. Then gently, her voice a light morning song, she coaxed the cloak from the tinsmith's shoulders. With her gaze on Giles only, she went to him. He dipped forward and she reached up to cover him with the cloak.

Beyond the cheers for Giles' freedom, came the rattle of an oxcart. Judgement would soon be upon them, for the reverend was near and he would escort all those branded as witches to the gallows.

Jameson turned back for the manor. Time was now urgent to grant Elizabeth's freedom, lest a question remain about her innocence, as he feared it would, for despite the innocence of Giles, those gathered believed their eyes had proved her guilt. The midwife passed him as he climbed the stairs, and he directed her to make haste in clothing Giles.

He stopped beside Elizabeth. "I will have your eyes here!" he called. "And I will know…" he touched his hand to Elizabeth's back, guided her down the stairs, not waiting a moment longer to present his decree, "who will clothe this innocent woman?"

No one stirred except the midwife and Abigail as they assisted Giles. The crowd silent, staring, stumbling backward as Jameson neared them with Elizabeth, as though to stand close to her would cause them great harm.

"I call for clothing!" He would see her dressed and mingled within the crowd, or well beyond, before the reverend entered the yard.

The first rumble came from the mob. A shout of disbelief. So contagious in its vehemence, others shouted the same.

"She bore the mark!" they cried, some with fury, others with fear. "'Twas there, upon her leg!"

"'Tis no mark of the beast," he said. "Had it been so, Giles would be marked as well. 'Tis my vow he is not."

Their grumbling continued, a discourse for which there was no time.

"Dawn has come!" he said, and the fate of those words threatened to close his throat so they might not be spoken. "Clothe this woman!"

The click of horse hooves and the creek of the cart drew the attention of those gathered toward the gate. Reverend John Cotton had arrived.

"Fear not, Elizabeth." Jameson spoke the words softly, assuringly, even as concern tightened his chest.

Animated greetings and praises came from the crowd as they parted to permit the reverend to pass, his step lively, almost gleeful, as he tread toward the manor.

Jameson held up his hand, silencing all, then tipped his head toward the reverend.

"Governor Foster." Cotton's own nod was more like a twitch. Though not a man of small stature, his eyes reached no higher than Jameson's own nose. His face was not one of charm, yet his form was impressive to more than a few, and his voice drew many to whatever cause he espoused.

He turned to Elizabeth, his gaze sweeping her body, showing neither interest nor disdain.

"Pity," he said with no regret whatsoever, clearly assuming guilt as she still stood unclothed.

With a lift of his hand and a flick of two fingers, he called his driver forward. Shackles clanked angrily in the man's hands, rattling some in the crowd as well. They gasped, their hands to their mouths. Others showed eager anticipation, while Elizabeth uttered a small desperate cry of alarm.

Jameson moved to stand before her, stopping the driver and reverend with a pointed look to each.

"This woman is unmarked by the beast," he said to them, and to all. "By my decree, she is innocent. There be no witches here in Wedick. You will leave here empty-handed today."

A hush, like that before a storm, fell over the crowd as all eyes settled on him. Cautious. Disbelieving. Then voices rose, not in healthy debate but in anger, rallying against his decree. Decrying his word as nonsensical, as they had witnessed the mark appear upon her. Some in the crowd pointed at her, called her a witch. Others huddled close to those beside them, fear in their eyes.

"Elizabeth's heart is pure," he said, and drew a steadying breath, presenting calm within himself so he might calm them. "As you witnessed, with your own eyes, the scuff upon her flesh..." He carefully strode through the crowd, turning his back to the men near Elizabeth, not permitting them to know of his concerns for her, "...I witnessed a lightness within her."

He let his gaze fall upon the gazes of those nearest to him. Showing them no hint of doubt. "I have examined many," he said. "Some whom I have examined you had feared, until I proved them to be unmarked." He nodded as he spoke and one or two nodded with him, hearing his words well. "So it be for Elizabeth," he said.

Without a glance toward Cotton, he went back to Elizabeth. Stood next to her, a hand reassuring to her and to them, upon her back. "A heart grows black once the body bears the devil's mark," he said. "The heart of Elizabeth Hobbs, on my word, is untouched by such evil."

They debated among themselves, some appeased, others unconvinced.

"I will see this mark, Foster." Cotton strode closer, his hands clasped low at his back, his gaze steady on Elizabeth. "Display it for me."

Jameson skirted a glance toward Giles, saw the tight set of his jaw, his rigid posture. Then Jameson turned to Elizabeth. Though he wished for a way to avoid subjecting her to such scrutiny yet again, it would be best for them to see this mark, for it had faded, as well it should.

"Elizabeth," he said, and locked his gaze on her horrified one. "You must."

Her trembling chin lifted, her lips set in a tight thin line. She reached a hand to her thigh, turned her leg to the side, displaying herself, her womanhood, her inner thigh, clearly and fully before all.

Pride stiffened her back even as a tear slipped from her eyes, eyes that challenged and dared as Cotton neared her, his spectacles in place as he all but buried his face against her sex.

Elizabeth tensed when he touched her. His fingers, cold no doubt, dabbling over the bruise. Her proud stance holding, though Jameson wished her to display humility instead.

"'Tis a mark, indeed." Cotton stood then, straightening slowly, as though soaking in the sight of her as well he could before turning away. Her beauty clearly undeniable even to one who believed her touched by evil. "Your eyes fail you, Governor, for I see it plain."

"I see it as well, Reverend. I have seen it and have examined it closely many times this hour past." He turned to the crowd. "Who among you discovered this mark upon Elizabeth?"

Mary came forward, her step hesitant. "'Twas my own eyes," she said.

A watcher, along with Samuel, Mary had been charged with assuring no familiar joined Elizabeth while she remained bound to the great oak. Her manner was gentle, though easily influenced was she by the virulence of the mob.

"Be true to your eyes once again," he said to her, his tone gentle, his hand more so upon her elbow as he guided her toward Elizabeth. "This mark has faded as wounds are want to do, has it not?"

Elizabeth's gaze, wary as Mary approached, turned soft, pleading.

Jameson gave a light squeeze to Mary's arm. Spoke softly to her as she peered closely at Elizabeth while kneeling before her. Her face, her hands, closer to Elizabeth's sex than even Cotton's had been.

"Is this a mark uncommon to your eyes, Mary?" he asked.

Her hand covered Elizabeth's on Elizabeth's thigh. She poked at the mark, dragged a finger over it, toward the crook where Elizabeth's thigh met her womanhood.

Elizabeth made not a sound, her gaze lowered to Mary, her body trembling, and Jameson could say naught to comfort her. Could only wait, respond in her defense, in defense as well of his decree, should the crowd be unconvinced even by Mary's word.

"I saw this as we examined her upon the platform," Mary said, and Jameson presented his hand to help her rise. "It is well-faded now," she said, "for it was a bright red spot when first I spied it."

"Did she resist your touches, Mary?" he asked strolling to stand behind Elizabeth. "Or the touches from the others here?"

"Nay."

'Twas their own eyes they trusted, and so it would be their own eyes he would convince once again.

He tipped his head toward Elizabeth's, aware she would seek to fight his hands upon her, yet upon her they would be. Now. Again. Here before all.

"Forgive," he said softly to her, and touched his hands to her waist. He held her still as she flinched and released one ragged breath after another. With the lightest caress against her chilled flesh, he swept his hands upward and cupped her soft full breasts.

"Did she respond, Mary?" He looked at the others, saw their eyes upon his hands, molding Elizabeth's breasts as he kneaded, squeezed, held them aloft. Her body rocked against his, in time, as though to a rapid pulse. "Did she sigh?" he asked softly. "Her body flush?"

He smoothed his hands forward and worked his fingers over her nipples, coaxing them to life with light flicks and pinches. "Did she shiver…alight and alive from your caresses alone, as now from my own hands?"

"Aye." Mary, too, watched his hands. Her gaze remaining there as she spoke. "'Twas, too, the same flush upon her chest then as now. Her face aflame as well."

He looked down at Elizabeth from behind as he milked her nipples with his fingers. The flush upon her face grew nearly as red as her hair.

"She is aflame with desire resisted," he said caressing her still, "for despite the shame of these examinations, she feels. Passion. Desire. All easily sated for her as well, unlike the witch. This I know, I witnessed, as did all of you. Did you not?"

He waited for their response, wished for one so it might leave no doubt, yet it did not come, mere murmurs did only. He stroked a hand lower, to rouse Elizabeth further, to rouse them as well.

He buried his fingers between her nether lips, aware of her panicked breaths, pleased by them for the crowd should see she did not seek this, as would Mercy, but resisted. Yet desire mounted. Beyond her control it was. They would see that as well and know she answered only to nature.

"Did you or did you not witness her passion?" he asked again, his voice louder, his fingers seeking her core, lightly stroking her, forcing pleasure upon her before all. "As we witness passion from her now?" He took his hand from her, his fingertips wetted for all to see.

"Aye," they answered, many still leering at her, others with eyes averted.

"'Tis clear, then," he said, easing away from her, "'twas your hands which placed this mark upon her..." He stood beside her, not blocking her from their view. "...for darkness resides nowhere upon her, neither upon her flesh nor upon her heart."

With a tip of his head, he invited Mary to stand back with the others, then he turned to Giles. Went to his friend.

"Of this I am convinced, for Elizabeth submitted herself, her pride set aside so she might spare Giles the shame of my examination." He pressed a hand to Giles' shoulder. "'Twas the same for Giles, as he came forward for her, each of them displaying a pureness of heart not shared by the witch."

Cotton stepped forward, his gait unhurried as he strode to Elizabeth.

Jameson remained where he was, wishing to stop the man in his tracks, yet wishing also not to be seen as defending her overmuch.

Cotton slapped his hand to Elizabeth's core. She cried out, a look of horror upon her face.

Giles lurched forward, and Jameson held him back, blocked him with his own body. Not permitting him to present a challenge he could not overcome.

Cotton flexed his hand, his entire arm. Clearly probing Elizabeth deeply. Her brows crimped, her eyes filled with fire.

"She is not a witch?" he asked, withdrawing his hand abruptly, leaving her trembling, wracked by shuddering breaths of shame and fury.

Though Cotton did not face him, Jameson squared his shoulders. "Nay."

Cotton pressed his fingers to his own nose and mouth, inhaled. Then he brushed his hand, back and forth, over Elizabeth's breast as though cleaning her scent from himself.

She looked only at him, directly, not speaking, not withdrawing, but accepting his vulgar gestures. Gestures Jameson detested yet knew well from this man.

He stepped toward Cotton, unwilling to permit yet more.

Cotton faced him, the move slow, precise. "None in your care be witches?"

"Nay."

"Why might that be, Foster?"

Jameson stopped where he was. Midway between Giles and Elizabeth. Facing Cotton. The crowd silent now as though breaths were held.

"If she who bears a mark," Cotton said with the wave of a contemptuous hand toward Elizabeth, "be not a witch… then who?"

"None this moon."

"Nor last." Cotton strolled closer to Jameson, closing the space between them.

Jameson remained in place, not easily intimidated even by the likes of this man, the most powerful voice for fear. Yet now he felt an unsteady beat within his chest. Unfamiliar it was, this beat he could not tame. His concern roused yet higher, for should the crowd still wish to condemn Elizabeth, he could do little more to convince them otherwise.

Cotton studied him, his head tilted back. An arrogant grin twisting his lips.

Jameson waited. Studied Cotton in return. His own gaze lowered to the man, his own lips pressed tight. Not sharing Cotton's conceit.

"Why, in months past..." Cotton clasped his hands at his back, turned away from Jameson, paced before him, his glance going toward the crowd, "and this month as well, have you not presented any for justice?" He stopped a good distance from Jameson. His stride purposeful, taking him among the people. As though his question came not from himself but from all gathered there. "Be your village so pure, so free of evil not one heart beating within it be blackened?"

Jameson loathed this vile man and the paranoia he sowed, preying on the faint hearts and deep fears of all those he encountered.

He kept his own step as nonchalant as Cotton's. Drew near the man. "Two have been banished this night," he said. "Their hearts, though not blackened, opened readily to the temptations of flesh." He fixed his gaze on Cotton's, a steady probing that made the man swallow audibly. "You know well of Mercy and Hannah Paine. Do you not, Reverend?"

With the speed of a rising sun, a flush of red mottled Cotton's neck and face. The truth of his own lusts for the women plain to all, lest the observer be blind.

Jameson steadied his gaze upon the flush, then captured Cotton's once again. Held it, so Cotton might know he kept no secrets. "'Tis they who I have sent far from here."

Cotton's jaw flexed but he did not speak.

"Not one in our village bears the devil's mark," Jameson said. "Not one deserves the noose." He drew a long slow breath, calmed some by Cotton's silence. He turned from the man then, looked at the others and called out, "This woman is an innocent among us! I will see her clothed!"

"You will see her clothed?" Cotton laughed, an absurd sound of mockery. "This woman all believe a witch?" He stepped toward Jameson, closing the gap. "You would release her?"

Jameson remained in place. His gaze lowered to him. "I would not see innocence punished."

"Innocence." Cotton nodded as though weighing the word. "You insist, Governor, that hearts here be not blackened. You banish whores, as well you should, as though said banishment should appease us all." He waved his hand in a high and grand sweep through the air. "As to imply evil has been routed from this place with their expulsion." He turned to the crowd as some acknowledged his words. "A whore tempts," he said. "Yet a whore, unmarked, is not a servant of Satan." He breathed deeply, his chest expanding as though filled by the shouts of agreement from the crowd. "A whore is not a witch!"

They all drew together behind him, around him, as one. His words, his passion driving their madness. Reawakening their thirst for blood. Mercy's banishment, Hannah's, no longer enough for them.

Jameson glanced back at Elizabeth. Wishing as much to whisk her away as throttle her for her earlier resistance, for had she submitted as had the others, she would have never been marked by the vile hands of this crowd. And Cotton would have no cause to rally all against sanity.

He faced Cotton. "No matter how sure your will," Jameson said, and he felt the power of his own voice rumble from his chest, "or that of the sheriff, the magistrates..." He strode among the people as Cotton had, drawing their attention back to himself, "…no matter the desire of any here…I will not send an innocent to the gallows." He listened past the shouts of disgust, heard some calls for calm and took heart. "As I have found only fear, shame…and innocence…beneath my hand, with each of these examinations, I commit no one to that fate."

"No one." Cotton did not shout yet all quieted and turned back to him. "Not now," Cotton said. "Not ever."

"Three moons ago," Jameson said. "I convicted two."

"Murderers they were, not witches," Cotton said. "Do you not believe we are tempted by darkness, Foster? Do you not believe hearts have been turned against goodness?" He wound a new path through the crowd, infecting them with his confident air and hateful words. "Do you not believe there be witches among us?" He stood in the center of all, a striking figure, seeming taller, broader, with all eyes upon him.

"I believe what my eyes do see," Jameson said, hoping common sense would ring truer than paranoia. "Should they show me a witch, I will say it be so. Yet I will not call a woman a witch simply because there might be witches about."

"Yet they are about in other villages," Cotton said. "Each month, I collect them. Each insisting on innocence. Yet their marks are seen, their hearts black. Their crimes often apparent with no effort required to prove them true." He strode through the crowd, his gaze well ahead, seeming not to see them as they parted to permit his passage, his step taking him back toward Jameson. "And here, time after time, there are none and I would know why. We would all know why!" He raised his hands as though appealing to all and they cried out together, demanding an answer. "Be it your heart, as well, has darkened, Governor?"

They gasped as one and turned to Jameson. Some backing away from him, others shouting against these foul words, for Cotton now dared to question not only Jameson's decree, but his honor...and his very soul.

"What faith have you in a governor who finds only...lightness of heart..." Cotton said, "...while other governors provide proof of darkness? Of witches." He spun toward the people with a flourish of his cloak, gesturing with his arms and his hands. "Perhaps he, himself, has made a pact with the devil!"

Screams and shouts filled the air, most in agreement, some in dissent, nearly drowning the sound of Cotton's voice, growing louder as he spoke, the hearts of so many seeming to blacken with his every word.

"Perhaps the devil's mark mars some secret spot upon your Governor's body." He shouted above the crowd, riled they were now as was clearly he wish. "For his heart seems most impure...perhaps deceiving all those who trust him most!"

Terror and fury colored the faces around Jameson. He stood taller among them, surrounded by them. His word, valued on so many occasions, never questioned this way, as though tainted by evil itself. He searched for Abigail, wondered whether her face would hold the same look of betrayal now as before. Now as on all the others there.

He spotted her. Near Giles. Tears in her eyes. Shaking her head no, a hand to her chest.

Giles called to the reverend in that moment, his voice thundering above the rest. Fury lit his eyes, stiffened his back and tightened the firm set of his jaw yet further. Yet he maintained a slow, leisurely pace as he strode toward the reverend, gaining for himself the attention of all, their voices quieting.

"Were I to accuse you, Sir," Giles said and the gentleness of his tone belied the rage Jameson recognized within him, "would that a witch make you?"

Cotton opened his mouth to respond and Giles snatched a woman from the group, silencing him.

Giles hauled the woman before him, ignoring the shouted objections and demands for her release.

"Should I say she be a witch..." he said, "this woman who stood among you...would you have her neck?" He snatched her face between his fingers. "Because I say she is a witch, be it so?"

Terror contorted the woman's features, and Jameson thought to reach for her, demand Giles release her at once, despite his good intent.

"'Tis not true," she cried, her eyes appealing to those before her. "I am not a witch. I am not!"

It was plain she was not, yet some in the crowd gasped and looked on in revulsion, while others insisted Giles unhand her.

His stand softened and he caressed his hand to her face. He stood behind her then, his hands set upon her shoulders. "She is not a witch," he said most softly. "She is not." He looked at everyone, then steadied his gaze on Cotton. "Yet with a few more words you would believe it so...much more than you would believe she is not." He looked at the others again with a compelling mix of confidence and anger in his eyes. "And you would readily condemn her," he said, "as you condemn Elizabeth. As you nearly condemn your governor."

He handed the trembling woman back to those with whom she had stood. "Would you see them hanged? Would you cheer their demise? All of you who could easily be accused as well?" His voice grew bold. A thick, gruff bark of words. And the crowd responded with both denials and affirmations. "Who then would be innocent?" he said. "Who then not?"

He moved along the edge of those gathered, not fitting himself between them. "And you now dare disparage our governor's honor as well? An examiner whose hand leaves not the brutal scars of torture...as upon my own flesh..." He ripped the cloak from his shoulders, wore not his jerkin only breeches, and turned his back to them, his cruel scars plain in the morning light. Their cries an undeniable release of shock and pity. "...flesh flayed in my youth," he said, "so I might confess against another..." He donned the cloak again and Jameson felt the struggle within Giles, having kept this secret all these years and now revealing it to all, on his behalf, "but a hand most patient, providing caresses meant to please. Touches meant to test the flesh for sensitivity when the devil would leave it numb. To rouse even the most timid..."

Giles clapped a hand to the shoulder of an elder man beside him. "Imagine your wife, Sir. Your daughter, accused. She would be stripped until bare..." He spoke over the gasps from around him as though they had not been uttered. "...shaved until nothing remained between her and her examiner."

Disgust filled eyes, scrunched faces, as though Giles' words somehow brought news to these people...yet Cotton stood unmoved.

"Which hand would you seek to examine her?" Giles said, and lifted his own hand in Jameson's direction. "The hand of our governor...or the hand of cruelty? Would you question his word then, when you trusted it before? Or would you believe in him and his decree? I ask you, whose hearts are dark? Whose are light?" He turned to Cotton then, and said no more.

Jameson had never questioned the depth of Giles' heart, nor the pride and power of the man. Yet to have such passion put forth on his behalf, to be defended with such vigor, was to have his own heart thrust into his throat.

He breathed only. Deeply. Unwilling to rouse the crowd in any way, but to allow Giles' words to settle well into their hearts. And then it seemed, with a collective breath, they had heard the depth of his plea to them and he had touched them as he had touched Jameson himself.

Jameson turned back to where Abigail had stood. Wished to feel her strength, even if only a fraction as that from Giles. She looked at him, as in awe, her heart no doubt as moved, as full as his own. Love, passion, lightness such as that deserved to be seen and heard and cherished. Not smothered by darkness brought on by malice and fear.

He stepped through the crowd then, his grateful gaze on Giles' shifting to those all about.

"Can your eyes not see innocence?" He asked softly. "Can your hearts?" He went to his friend, stood shoulder to shoulder beside him. "What proof will satisfy you? The flaying of flesh as for our Giles? And what proves guilt?" He felt the eyes upon him soften. The minds willing, at least, to hear reason. And he drew a breath, encouraged by those he had doubted, those who moments ago rallied against him.

"I say 'tis no more than your fear will do that!" he said. "I will not feed that fear just to satisfy it, for a morsel does not slake the appetite for blood, it riles it! It teases it until it craves yet more, as has been proven here."

He looked at Abigail as she drew near, at the tears in her eyes, tears he wished to dry, to never see there again. "My word is my honor," he said to her as to all. "I will not speak words meant to appease, but speak truth, even should it be unpleasant."

He turned to Cotton, daring the man to challenge him now as all stood in rapt attention to his words. "And the truth this night, this moonset. This new day…" Jameson said to all, "…is innocence for all those in my care, all those who suffered so greatly by cruel accusations. They are all free of the devil's mark. Innocent! That is my word. Should you not believe, have no faith that I speak truth, then I offer my own neck." Their objections were boisterous and he shouted over them. "Here and now! Without quarrel, I will go with the reverend, to the gallows! Be that what you seek?"

They shifted about, cries of shock, of supplication resounding around him. And then Mary took a hesitant step from the crowd and they quieted, turned to look at her as she moved to stand beside him, facing the reverend. William Wildes, leaning upon his cane, hobbled forward, his step slow, unsteady, yet sure to Jameson's other side, near Giles. The midwife came forward. The old cobbler, the woman Giles had drawn from the crowd. Martha Farrington - church elder, accused and proven innocent by his hand just hours ago…

Then he turned to the reverend as well, pleased such fairness and reason had returned to the hearts of his neighbors. He looked at Abigail, standing now nearly alone as the others came round him. Her gaze rested on his. Tenderness there. Fear. Reassurance. Her step through the others was slow at first, then confident.

He had to swallow twice so he might feel his throat, so dry and tight it was. She stopped before him and he felt the heat of her. Smelled her scent, wanted to wrap her in his arms. Assure her as her eyes sought to assure him.

"Abigail," he said in a whisper, his gaze never leaving hers.

"Jameson." She breathed his name and it was as though she shouted it from the manor stairs, so deeply did it touch him.

Cotton stormed toward them. "'Tis madness!" He waved a finger to all beside Jameson. "Evil has filled your hearts, so well, you cannot see it." He pointed at Elizabeth, proud yet frightened, she remained as stone before the manor stairs. "There is evil here in Wedick Colony." Cotton marched past those gathered around and reached Jameson. "You, sir...I will have your neck, for I do not believe your word. These people do not believe your word."

Their own words, shouted at the reverend, the thrust of them toward him, fingers pointing, rage flowing, belied his words on their behalf. Their voices near as one in denial, though some broke free and stood beside Cotton, most remained at Jameson's side.

Jameson pitied the others, the terror coursing through their veins, fueled so well by Cotton's words. Words that poured fear into so many hearts.

Jameson took a step closer to the man, then took another. "Evil is found when evil is sought," he said, "and you, Sir, seek it as readily as you draw air." He took yet another step, nearly standing upon the reverend's toes. "Here, in my village, in this village we love and call our home... there has never been evil such as that of which you speak...until now."

Murmurs of agreement rippled around him.

Cotton's eyes--filled with rage now, rage and something else--widened and he thrust his arm out before him, pointing past Jameson to Elizabeth. "It lies within her! 'Tis she who strikes fear in the hearts here..." He went toward her, pushing his way through the crowd. "From my arrival, all here cried against your word of her innocence!" He snatched her hair in his fist, pulled her head backward, ignored her cry. "Her face, these eyes of green, this hair...fire!" He released her, ran his hands over her, nowhere and everywhere. "She is well adorned when she should be modest. She compels the eye in lustful ways that blind men to truth--as is the witch's way." He closed a hand over her arm and pulled her into the crowd.

To Jameson's great relief, they did not stand back but remained in place behind him, beside him, around him, not cowering from Elizabeth now.

"She bears a mark upon her," Cotton said, "undenied by all! How did you test it, Foster? With your tender touches? Is that all?" He looked past Jameson, called out to his driver. "From the cart," he said, "my etwee! Bring it here at once!"

Incredulous, Jameson could only look on, for despite his impudence and guile, Cotton would not dare do as implied. Witch hunters, alone, carried their tools with them, the reverend should not carry the same. Yet Cotton was unlike most others, vile and vengeful, his way being whichever advanced his cause and his lofty position among the masses.

Jameson waited, almost wishing it would be as he thought, for only then, with evidence plain for all to see, would the depth of this madness be clear for all.

"The witch's mark," Cotton said, dragging Elizabeth behind as he wove his way further through the people, "placed there by Satan himself, will not bleed. And now we shall see how true that be for this woman, accused and marked so well."

Unwilling was Jameson to allow Cotton occasion to harm Elizabeth, though he knew to his gut, that was Cotton's intent.

Jameson followed him, Giles not far behind, the crowd parting for the pair of them.

The driver returned and reached Cotton two steps before Jameson. Giles stopped beside Elizabeth.

The wooden box retrieved from the cart was as long as a man's foot. Flowers, intricately carved, adorned the exterior. The fabric within, a bold blue, was like that of a winter night sky. A pincher with jagged teeth, and a pick sharpened to the longest, cruelest point lay nestled atop the fabric. Devious devices they were, as Jameson feared. Devices of other governors, other examiners, sheriffs, jailers, and constables. Devices meant to maim, to cause great fear and pain. Devices Jameson would not permit used on those in his care.

Cotton snatched the pick from its bedding, held it aloft. "I will prick the mark to be sure it bleeds, to be certain it is not a spot deadened to sensation…for that, my good people, is how to test the witch!"

Jameson snatched the vile tool from Cotton's hand, its sharpened tip more than a man's finger in length. He held it high for all to see. "This is what you seek? To have the accused tested this way? With iron pierced into their flesh so they might scream as their blood pours? Is that what you would have me do to the accused? Is that the examiner you seek?"

Their voices grew louder. As though all in the world shouted with them.

"Nay!"

Words shouted well above the rest, chided the reverend for his viciousness. The faces of all clear in this new light of day, their fear, their anger and their own desire for blood, unquenched now that he stirred it, leaving them still to thirst. Needing someone upon which to point their anger.

Jameson, as well, needed that someone, for that someone had caused strife and fear and cruel pain in the hearts of all he had examined, all who had stood with him, all who had before demanded Elizabeth's blood and now demanded punishment for the one who would draw it.

He looked at each within the crowd. Noted Giles with Elizabeth, the two looking on as only the other existed. Giles drew the cloak from his shoulders and wrapped it around hers, while all around them people shouted and pounded the air with their fists.

"If there be evil among us now..." Jameson said "...'tis one heart which houses it." He soaked in the screams and shouts around him, aware his words riled them more. Yet willing was he to take this chance. For reason, as with the sun, seemed to have now lit upon these people, giving him hope that the shock of this truth might replace madness with clarity. "'Tis in one who sees evil wherever he looks."

He looked at Cotton closely, saw the smug sense of disdain upon his face. Whether disdain for truth or for those who did not fall at his feet, Jameson did not know, and did not care to learn. "'Tis because he, himself, not those he accuses, has been blackened by it!"

Their cries and shouts grew louder. A deafening roar. The crowd gathered yet closer. Fists in the air. Fury in their eyes. Crowding closer still.

"Do you not see evil clearly?" Jameson said.

"Aye!"

"Would you see this evil routed?"

They were riotous now. Fueled by their lust for blood, his words and their own fears.

"Would you see the very vessel for the devil's work gone? Banished?" He drew words from deep in his gut, fury from deep in his own heart. The relentless brutality would end this night, he would see it be so. "Never to allow such evil to Wedick again?"

They crowded closer still, crushing in. A mob he could not tame should he try. Yet this time, this once, he would try not, for blackness such as had been brought to his village this night had never infiltrated hearts so fully as now.

Though neither compassion nor honor had routed evil before, perhaps evil itself would do so. "So many have been accused of allying with evil," Jameson said above the din, "and in answer, we display yet more! Stripping them of their clothes. Their dignity. Ripping them from their lives and their families. Hanging them!" He turned so all would see him, hear him, deny him not. "Tell me, who does this please? What feeds these actions? Love? Goodness? Or evil itself?"

He studied the faces of those nearest him. Challenged each with a long steady gaze. Ready to crush all dissent, all debate that might come from the crowd.

Yet none did, and he drew a breath, deep and satisfying, then bellowed above the cries from the crowd. "Would you see evil destroyed?"

A bone-chilling shout rose from all of them as from one. "Aye!"

"Never to permit its return?"

"Aye!"

"Then I ask…" He turned to the reverend, standing incredulous beside him and snatched him by the back of his neck. "And you will all answer this one final time…" He shoved the man toward mob, blood-lust clear in their eyes and in their hearts. "Be this a witch?"

Arla Dahl

The Watchman

About the Author

Arla Dahl is a lover and avid reader of all things sexy and suspenseful. In her Immoral Virtue Trilogy, the horrors of the 17th Century witch trials are exposed, examined and reversed. Deeply moved by the viciousness of times, Arla created stories that would turn history on its ear and make that which labeled the accused susceptible to the temptations of evil, into the one thing that would set them free. Lust.

Stay engaged!

Find Arla online

Facebook at www.facebook.com/arladahl

Twitter: https://twitter.com/ArlaDahlAuthor

Her blog: http://www.arladahl.com/notes/

See also, her website

www.arladahl.com

The Watchman

Some words from Arla

It started on a gray, frigid day in 1692. Two girls, aged 9 and 11, the reverend's daughter and niece, fell ill. Though not in any normal way. They screamed hateful and vile things, they convulsed, they fell silent and motionless…and neither shake, nor slap nor shout could rouse them.

Soon other girls fell ill as well.

Sick girls of various ages. Indian attacks. Poor weather, withered crops and smallpox.

All of this pointed to one cause.

The people in the village of Salem had somehow sinned, and in so doing had allowed Satan access to their hearts and souls. It had to be.

Who among them resisted? Who among them remained untouched? More importantly, who among them had been marked? Branded by the beast…

Who among them was a witch?

The afflicted girls accused many over the coming months. And, fearful for their own souls, pillars of the community as well as doltish neighbors, believed them.

The girls pointed to rafters, insisting specters of their tormentors, invisible to all eyes but theirs, hovered, mocked, pinched, chided. They did the devil's work, the girls said. They urged more to follow, to sign his evil book with their blood. To mate with him. To breed darkness.

Over the coming months, several men and dozens of women, poor or otherwise — mothers, daughters, grandmothers as well — were accused. They were questioned by the court. Imprisoned in filthy, dank, rat-, disease-, and insect-infested jails.

They were tortured with foul food, if any food at all, with lack of sleep... Stripped bare and chained. Fondled, probed – examined, it was said – by their jailors, by strangers. By evil itself. Privately. Publicly. It did not matter. It was all in the name of seeking the devil's mark...which all knew to be hidden in some private place upon the witch's body...

In a space of four months, nineteen people were hanged as witches, as well two dogs. One man was pressed to death. More awaited their turns, left to rot in jail...where some indeed did perish.

And then the governor's wife was accused. Her crime? Acting beyond her authority to grant the release of another woman imprisoned for witchcraft. Then a specter of the minister's wife appeared to someone...and since only a witch would have a specter...

Soon, an order was issued outlawing the use of spectral evidence. And soon after that, the governor dissolved the very court he had established just six months prior, a court formed solely to oversee the trials of accused witches.

The madness that flowed through Salem and its neighboring towns faded as more and more people of prominent standing were accused and thrown into jail.

As the heartfelt cries of innocence poured from the mouths of those about to be hung, more hearts softened and turned from the cause.

As quickly as it had begun, the hysteria ended. Many accused witches who had been condemned to hang, were eventually released or pardoned, though not before all they owned, all they knew and loved, had been ripped from them.

In 1693, Governor Phips pardoned some of those still imprisoned, many who were unable to pay fees accrued by their jailing. Years later, and decades later still, more of those who suffered so greatly were pardoned as well.

However, it would not be until three hundred years later, on October 31, 2001, when all those who had endured those unspeakable horrors, including those who had been left unnamed in past pardons—the final few accused, imprisoned or hanged—had their names and their sufferings recognized, honored, and added to the list of innocents so they might be fully and finally exonerated.

The accused witches of Salem could rest at last.

Yet, as they lay in their unmarked graves in New England, and as those who had gathered to remember them all these centuries later, said a prayer then turned away, fear, ignorance, mass hysteria and immoral virtue continue to bring suffering to innocents in villages around the world. Disease infests, crops fail, droughts occur. And people die.

For too many, it all points to one chilling cause. Someone among them must be a witch.

May you be unmarked,

Arla